SPECIAL MESSAGE TO READERS

THE ULVERSCROFT FOUNDATION
(registered UK charity number 264873)

was established in 1972 to provide funds for research, diagnosis and treatment of eye diseases. Examples of major projects funded by the Ulverscroft Foundation are:-

- The Children's Eye Unit at Moorfields Eye Hospital, London
- The Ulverscroft Children's Eye Unit at Great Ormond Street Hospital for Sick Children
- Funding research into eye diseases and treatment at the Department of Ophthalmology, University of Leicester
- The Ulverscroft Vision Research Group, Institute of Child Health
- Twin operating theatres at the Western Ophthalmic Hospital, London
- The Chair of Ophthalmology at the Royal Australian College of Ophthalmologists

You can help further the work of the Foundation by making a donation or leaving a legacy. Every contribution is gratefully received. If you would like to help support the Foundation or require further information, please contact:

THE ULVERSCROFT FOUNDATION
The Green, Bradgate Road, Anstey
Leicester LE7 7FU, England
Tel: (0116) 236 4325

website: www.foundation.ulverscroft.com

ENCHANTMENT IN MOROCCO

Stranded in Morocco, Emily Ryan accepts a job offer from a stranger. Entranced by her new life in the sleepy coastal village of Taghar, she struggles to resist widower Rafi Hassan's charm — but also clashes with his autocratic ways and respect for tradition. As she attempts to persuade him to allow his teenage daughter Nour more freedom, Emily refuses to acknowledge her own errors of judgement. As the seasons turn and the olives ripen, Emily dares to dream of winning Rafi's heart — until danger threatens from an unexpected quarter . . .

MADELEINE McDONALD

♦

ENCHANTMENT IN MOROCCO

Complete and Unabridged

LINFORD
Leicester

First published in Great Britain in 2010

First Linford Edition
published 2016

The characters and events in this book are
fictitious. Any resemblance to real persons,
living, or dead, is purely coincidental.

A catalogue record for this book is available
from the British Library.

ISBN 978–1–4448–3019–4

Published by
F. A. Thorpe (Publishing)
Anstey, Leicestershire

Set by Words & Graphics Ltd.
Anstey, Leicestershire
Printed and bound in Great Britain by
T. J. International Ltd., Padstow, Cornwall

This book is printed on acid-free paper

1

Abandoned by her driver, Emily Ryan sat alone in the hotel lounge. She checked her watch again, stifling the misgivings that plagued her. There was nothing to do except admire a large portrait of the King of Morocco, resplendent in white robes and a red fez. Already she had waited over an hour. It was bewildering not to understand anyone, and vexing not to speak a word of French or Arabic to ask what was happening.

The day had begun well. In the plane, Emily had craned her neck to look out of the window when the pilot announced they had begun the descent to Casablanca's Mohammed V International Airport. Her spirits soared as she caught a glimpse of the African coastline and she settled back in her seat. *Morocco, here I come!*

Adventure beckoned again. Emily had just finished an eighteen-month trip around

America, her father's homeland, and the prospect of temporary work while she found her feet again in grey, rain-soaked London held no appeal. When a chance recommendation led to the offer of a job in Morocco, it was the answer to her prayers.

She glanced around the almost-deserted lounge. What if something had happened to Madame Cherif, her new employer? What if no-one turned up to meet her? What if, what if? As another ten minutes ticked away, her mind spun scary scenarios.

On impulse, she reached into her bag and counted her cash. She had enough to cover a couple of nights in a hotel. Not this one, though. It would have to be a budget hotel. If no-one turned up soon, she would have to start looking for one.

She was no slouch at looking after herself in a strange city. Her American trip had shown her that. In the States she had found casual work as a waitress, chambermaid, receptionist or shop assistant in turn. A few weeks to put away some spare cash towards the next adventure: the next plane ticket, the next skiing weekend, the next sightseeing trip in a hot air balloon, the next stay at a wilderness lodge.

Bring it on! I've never been afraid of hard work. Emily suppressed the thought that here in North Africa, a foreigner — especially one who had to use sign language — would not find it so easy to walk into casual employment.

Don't be silly, she chided herself. She already had a job, as an informal language teacher. Her duties would be simple: to speak English to Madame Cherif's children. Although she had little experience of working with children, how difficult could that be?

She checked her watch again. Stifling mounting apprehension, she reminded herself that a driver had met her at the airport. Her employer would be along to meet her soon.

It was cool inside the hotel, in contrast to the brilliant sunshine outside. She curbed her impatience to walk out and explore the city. She had been driven here straight from the airport, with no opportunity to soak up new sights and smells — apart from the warmth that enveloped her as she followed her driver out of the air-conditioned arrivals hall. When Emily paused to remove her jacket, the breeze caressed her bare arms. Simply incredible: even the breeze was warm. *I must pinch myself*, she had thought. *This is real. It's all real.*

The driver who met her spoke no English, but the board he held had *Emily Ryan* written across it, and he mangled the pronunciation of her name as she approached him. He scurried off with her cases, leaving her to follow him to a large silver car. Then he abandoned her at the hotel, with a cheery smile but no word of explanation.

Think positive, she told herself. The reason she had been given the job was that she spoke only English. She took another cautious sip of the tiny glass of mint tea that the waiter had placed in front of her. It had gone cold and was far too strong for her taste, but she did not even know how to ask for something else.

My first taste of Africa. I have to expect things to be different.

'You have to put sugar in it.' The comment came from a stranger who sat down at her table uninvited. 'Europeans always make that mistake.'

Emily frowned at him. She was not worried about fending off advances from strange men, but the long wait had unsettled her. Where was Madame Cherif?

At the same time, she could not help noticing the powerful lines of his frame and the fluid ease of his movements. Although he was formally dressed in a linen suit, the image of a pirate commanding the quarterdeck of the ship he had just taken rose unbidden to Emily's mind. It was the single gold earring, she decided.

'I am waiting for someone.'

'That's right: me,' he replied. He spoke English; fluently, it seemed.

She looked down at her glass, using the moment to bring her errant thoughts under control, then focused again on her uninvited companion. But the buccaneer image etched on her mind refused to vanish. Instead, she became even more conscious of the intense green eyes in his dark face, and of the single earring below wiry hair. She returned his direct gaze and, as if in response, he leaned slightly toward her, hands clasped loosely on the briefcase in front of him.

In other circumstances she would have been tempted to make his acquaintance. To spend an agreeable half-hour keeping him at a safe distance while listening to whatever he chose to say in that silky, alluring accent. *Not here, not now,* she decided. Not when her new employer might walk in at any minute.

'I am waiting for Madame Cherif.' Annoyance that she had been unable to subdue an instinctive response to his presence made her tone glacial.

'Sofia is my cousin. She asked me to

meet you, Miss Ryan.'

Emily felt foolish, which fanned her anger. What right did this man have to barge in without introducing himself properly? What right did he have to distract her from her concerns with that roguish edge of seduction in his silky voice?

'Where is Madame Cherif?' At least he could tell her what was happening.

He laughed. 'At this moment, my dear cousin is running around like, how do you say, a legless chicken.'

'Headless chicken.' The words slipped out automatically, and the man laughed again, with a rueful shake of his head.

'I forgot you were a teacher. 'Headless chicken', I will remember. Now, would you like another glass of tea? And I will show you how it should be drunk.' He signalled to the waiter.

Emily was tempted. The relief of knowing she was in the right place weakened her resolve. Right place — right person — and he just happened to be gorgeous. It was a long time since a personable man had crossed her path. After the long journey, it would be pleasant to take time to relax with someone who seemed totally at ease with himself and his surroundings. Nor need she feel guilty about taking time out. Without prying, it would give her an opportunity to find out more about her new employer's household.

The man moved his slim leather briefcase to one side, and she caught a glimpse of the wedding ring on his left hand. *Story of my life. All the attractive men I meet are married.* Admittedly, this one's manner seemed forceful rather than flirtatious, but one never knew. In a strange country it was best to be prudent.

'No thank you.' She softened her refusal with a smile. 'I'd rather go and get settled in.'

'That, I am afraid, will not be possible.' The shock of his words did not sink in; and, seeing her bewilderment, he shrugged and spread his hands wide. 'My cousin sends her prolific apologies.

She attempted to contact you this morning, but you had already left for the airport.'

'Why? What's the problem?' Panic surged in Emily. This could not be happening.

'Sofia's husband, the engineer, must go to Dubai this weekend. There are technical problems which need to be fixed, you understand. The family go with him. So, Sofia runs like the headless chicken, organizing their departure. I am sorry, Miss Ryan, there is no job for you now.'

This time the words did reach her. There was no mistaking them, and the shock of his announcement blotted out her initial response to his powerful physical presence.

'I have a contract,' she retorted. That was not strictly true; all she had in her bag was a charming letter from Madame Cherif. It might not be a legal document, but surely it represented some sort of contract?

Emily had foreseen no problems in

9

accepting Madame Cherif's invitation to *become one of the family* for a few months. Why bother with the formality of proper work papers?

What have I done now? All her life, Emily's impetuous decisions had got her into scrapes, but she usually managed to turn them to her advantage. Now it seemed her luck had run out.

She sat up straight, ready to do battle. This man, whoever he was, could not just turn around and tell her the job was gone. He could not strand her in a foreign country.

'It is the shock for you, *n'est-ce pas?*' The words were sympathetic, but the tone perfunctory. Green eyes appraised her. Emily shifted in her seat under his scrutiny, uneasily conscious of her travel-rumpled clothes.

'My cousin gives me discretion to deal with her problem. So now I must decide what to do with you.'

Emily stifled a gasp of protest. It was bad enough to be described as a *problem*, but this stranger did not even intend to consult her about his plans for her future.

'What do you propose?' She endeavoured to keep her tone neutral.

'For tonight, you stay here in the hotel. Tomorrow, we shall see.' He paused and looked straight at her so that Emily felt the full force of his compelling gaze.

'Tomorrow?' Tomorrow meant that there was an alternative. She could not go back. She did not have a home to go to, for her belongings were still in storage. Boxes in a lock-up in London had been the last thing on her mind during her voyage of discovery around her father's homeland. She was not going back, not now.

He appeared to come to a decision. 'I offer you a job.' His tone brooked no refusal. 'In the south,' he added after a fractional pause, but the information meant nothing to Emily.

'As an English teacher?' Although there had been nothing untoward so far in his words or manner, she must keep her feet on the ground. What kind of offer would this stranger choose to make her? *It's the earring*, she decided, *it so makes him look like a pirate ready to take me captive.* Or maybe it was her own fancy to be taken captive that unleashed such wild imaginings. She must not let that distract her now.

A shadow passed over his face. 'Not exactly. My daughter needs a companion.' He fell silent for a moment, before adding, 'You may speak English to her as well.'

His reticence set warning bells clanging, but Emily chose to ignore them. Acting as companion to a little girl was a respectable occupation. She had already taken one gamble in coming here. Whatever was offered, she would make the best of it.

'What about my salary?' She blurted out the question before she realized how mercenary she sounded. Resentment surfaced when his face reflected surprise. *If you were in my shoes, that would be the first question you would ask too.*

Emily had killed two birds with one

stone in coming to Morocco. Employment in a sunny climate had to be better than a temporary position in bleak, damp London. To top it all, when Madame Cherif mentioned the munificent salary she offered, Emily's first reaction had been that in six months she could save enough to pay off her credit cards.

The total amount she owed the card companies was something she pushed to the back of her mind. A couple of missed payments when she was at a low ebb, and somehow matters had snowballed from there. *I'm maxed out*, she told herself after she received the first warning emails. At the beginning, *maxed out* had a comforting ring. The words sounded efficient, like a deliberate strategy rather than a catastrophe. Over the months, *maxed out* took on a more threatening sound, and a relentless tide of interest and penalties outran her efforts to pay off her debts. She dreaded opening the bills that arrived in her inbox each month.

Here in Morocco, she would have

been housed and fed. If she saved most of what she earned on top of her keep, her total debt would be manageable, not scary. Would this man be as generous as the Cherifs?

'I will pay whatever you agreed with Sofia. Unless, of course, you want more?'

For a mad moment, Emily was tempted. But his direct, questioning gaze flustered her. If she asked for more, she might see disdain in his eyes. Extra money did not seem worth the queasiness that threatened her stomach at the thought of earning his contempt.

'No, no, that's fine,' she babbled, relieved to have the matter settled. *Six months is all I need. I can do anything for six months.*

She brought her thoughts back to her companion. *Come on, Emily*, she chided herself. Making a poor impression on her new employer was the last thing she wanted. *Show interest in something other than money, or he will send you back on the next plane.*

'And your wife?' A wedding ring

advertised to the world that he was taken. 'Won't your wife want to interview me? Do excuse me; I don't even know your name.'

'My name is Hassan, Rafi Hassan. My wife died some years ago. It was a great sadness for my daughter.'

'I'm sorry.' Emily hesitated, unsure whether to say more. Words seemed inadequate in such a situation. Formal condolences were inappropriate years after the event, and she could hardly change the subject.

That explained the wedding ring, though. She shot an involuntary glance at his left hand. He had lean, shapely hands, but there was something not quite right about them. The puzzle tugged at Emily's mind.

She wondered if he still wore his ring by choice or by custom. Emily knew little of wedding-ring etiquette. As a twelve-year-old, she had witnessed her mother throw her own into the Thames when her father left them. Looking back, she dated the start of her quarrels with her mother to that ill-fated outing.

'Good riddance,' Mum spat as she watched the murky water claim it. 'Don't you dare turn out like your wastrel of a father.'

Emily had cried herself to sleep that night.

Then again, just now Rafi Hassan had spoken of his daughter's sadness, not his own. Emily guessed a youngish, attractive widower would soon find consolation, in any country. She stole a sideways glance at him, seeking the answer. No doubt about it, the man was gorgeous, although he appeared unaware of his effect on her. A man so at ease with himself must have someone in his life, she decided. She wondered whether the offer of a job sprang from concern for his daughter, or from a desire to pack her out of the way. Emily felt for the motherless child, knowing what it was like to grow up with a single parent who could not wait to be rid of her.

'Tell me more about your daughter. What's her name?'

His face softened. 'You will like her. She is called Nour. It is a traditional name that signifies 'light'.'

'That's charming.' Emily was struck by the way his voice changed. There was warmth in his tone that had not been there before. So he did care. 'How old is she?'

'Seventeen last month.'

Thrown off-balance by his answer, it took a second to regain her footing. He did not look anywhere near old enough to have a seventeen-year-old daughter. A small child she could handle; a grown girl would be different.

'But ... that's almost grown-up. Surely I ought to meet her first?'

Think before you speak. Don't throw this chance away.

Rafi waved her objection aside. 'Nour will do as I say.'

Emily sat silent, digesting his reply. Rafi stood abruptly. 'I have an appointment. I leave you now, and I will make arrangements for you to travel tomorrow.' He reached across the table to shake her hand, the touch of his fingers firm against her palm for a brief moment. 'Goodbye, Miss Ryan.'

Left to ponder her misgivings, it annoyed her how he had taken her consent for granted: disregarding her concern for his daughter's feelings, and overriding her half-hearted objection. Clearly her new employer was a man accustomed to being obeyed. *Beggars can't be choosers*, she told herself. A job was a job, her travels had taught her that, and this job offered her a chance to wipe the financial slate clean. Her stomach clenched as she remembered her debts.

She walked to the window, and caught a glimpse of deep turquoise sea beyond the palm trees that fringed the road. Her money worries would not vanish overnight, but in this magical land they somehow seemed less pressing. She remembered how her spirits lifted as she stepped into the warmth and sunlight beyond the airport's arrivals hall. Lastly, there was Rafi Hassan. High-handed he might be, but Emily's interest was piqued.

Bumping her fists together to seal the bargain, she turned away from the view and walked to the desk to check in.

Later that night, it occurred to her that Rafi Hassan had the hands of a workman. That was what had puzzled her, healing scratches on the smooth, dark skin of his otherwise well-kept hands. On that image, she fell asleep.

★ ★ ★

The drive south was interminable. Another driver collected her in the morning. At first, Emily sat tense on the edge of her seat, convinced they would have an accident. The driver exhausted his few words of English, leaving her to sip from her water bottle and watch buses and trucks jostle for road space with overburdened donkeys. Yet somehow no-one came to grief, not even the moped riders who buzzed through the dense traffic like angry mosquitos.

Hours passed. They left the coast and

climbed into the hills in long, looping coils. Now and again she glimpsed a snow-covered summit in the far distance, the view immediately cut off again. Emily stared in wonder, having always imagined Morocco to be a desert country.

At midday, the driver ushered her into another large hotel, and vanished. Emily caught a glimpse of the main dining room, dominated by another imposing portrait of the King. A respectful waiter settled her in a private alcove, leaving Emily to nibble at a salad platter of lettuce, sliced oranges and sliced egg topped with stuffed green olives.

The mint tea that accompanied the meal brought to mind the first words Rafi Hassan had spoken to her. A comment she had dismissed as a chat-up line until he revealed his identity. Remembering now, she added sugar to the tea, surprised to find the contrast between sweet and strong refreshing. There was so much she did not know yet. She had had no time to read about Morocco before her hasty departure to meet the

Cherifs. Now there would be other customs to learn.

The image of Rafi Hassan explaining the ways of his country, seated across the table in the forced intimacy of a private alcove, sent an odd prickle down her spine.

She shut out the strangely enticing image of the two of them closeted together. *I don't need him. I've got six months. Plenty of time to find out the way things are done.*

She had dreamed of Rafi. In her dream his green eyes smiled. As he held his hand out for her, the scene dissolved into a mocking sea of sand dunes. *It was only a dream*, she told herself, annoyed that she even remembered it — annoyed that the man should invade her thoughts night and day. She dismissed her imaginings, and instead smiled her thanks at the waiter who came to clear the table.

When the car rejoined the coast road, the warm air, combined with the light meal and the fatigue of the journey, made it impossible to stay awake. She dozed off, waking every now and then at changes in the car's rhythm. Eventually the driver pulled up, turned around to her and pointed. 'Taghar,' he said.

Down below, buildings formed a huddle at the water's edge. Shapes were indistinct in the dusk, but she identified the minaret that rose above the huddle, its turquoise roof-tiles glinting in the setting sun. To each side of the village a beach curved around a small bay.

She wanted to tell the driver to wait, allowing her to comb her hair and apply fresh lipstick. But already he had put the engine in gear and the car was nosing its way down. As he opened the door for her, she smelled salt in the air and heard the rhythmic smack of the ocean encountering the shore.

As dusk thickened, she was ushered into a walled courtyard and left alone. She scrabbled in her bag and located her lipstick and comb. The girl might not notice, but it made Emily feel better.

When Nour came into the courtyard to greet her, Emily detected a resemblance to her father in her hair and eyes. In contrast to Rafi's breezy confidence, Nour entered hesitantly. She spoke to Emily in slow, careful English, looking down at a letter she held in her hand. 'My father writes I must make you welcome, Miss Ryan.' The words were stiff, as if rehearsed.

'Emily, please, you may call me Emily.' The friendly words died on her lips as Nour looked up from her letter and directed a hostile gaze at her.

2

Rafi arrived a week later. In the intervening days, Emily had schooled herself to forget him. The thought of his arrival aroused trepidation.

Nour was uncooperative and sullen, making it clear when she showed Emily round the tiny village that she did so out of obligation. Emily was doubly isolated, since the housekeeper, Meriam, spoke no English, but kept watch on their comings and goings through the open kitchen door.

Despite Emily's repeated overtures, Nour often vanished, leaving Emily to explore alone. *What have I got myself into?* Emily asked herself day after day. On solitary walks on the wide, grassy terraces above the village, she marvelled at the pale canopies of almond blossom, heady with fragrance, and the massive, gnarled trunks of the olive trees. But they never distracted her attention for long.

Speaking with Rafi in Casablanca, she had thought only of finding a solution to her financial predicament. Convinced by the warmth in his voice, she sensed his daughter was the chink in his armour. That had seemed another good reason to accept the job. Here in Taghar, however, she decided that Rafi could have little empathy with his only child if he expected her to welcome a stranger.

In counterpoint to her doubts was the memory of the confident man she had met, the man with an edge of impudence that added to his charm. A memory that came to mind all too often — although she did her best to suppress it. A dalliance with her employer, however enticing the thought, was not on the agenda.

It was impossible to contact Rafi by telephone. Taghar was too remote ever to have had landlines, and mobile phones did not work down in the bay.

Emily fretted. The days passed, and still Rafi sent no message. Whenever she thought of him, which was often, she reminded herself that the only reason she wished to speak to him was to clarify the terms of her employment.

'What exactly am I supposed to do here?' she asked Nour a few days into her stay.

There was a wary look in the girl's face. 'In my father's letter, he says you will be my friend.'

Emily felt an unexpected wave of sympathy. Bad-mannered and grouchy she might be, but who could blame her when her father behaved in such an autocratic way? Girls of that age back home would be thinking about getting a job or going to college, and this one's father had imposed a governess on her.

I wouldn't have wanted a nanny at seventeen. Emily had sensed that something was wrong when Rafi Hassan had offered her the job, but she allowed him to override her doubts. Now Nour did not want her as a companion.

'I guess we're stuck with each other until your father returns,' she told Nour. 'When will that be?'

Nour's face crumpled. 'I never know. I am girl. Papa, he never talk to me about the business, but I know he is much busy now.'

Looking at her woebegone face, Emily's sympathy became tinged by impatience. Clearly, Rafi could not run a business without access to modern telecommunications, and that might explain his frequent absences. It was odd that Nour did not understand. Emily wondered if the girl was simply going through a teenage phase of being misunderstood, and dramatizing her feelings to suit that scenario.

Sensing her change of mood, Nour withdrew, leaving Emily sitting alone in the courtyard. *If I had any sense, I'd be out of here next week*, she mused.

As if! Her financial situation mocked her. A small bird landed on the table to peck at the crumbs. She did not bother to chase it away. 'I've nowhere else to go,' she told the bird. 'Six months is all

I need. I'll have to sit it out here till then.' She batted away the thought that six months in Rafi's company would be no hardship.

* * *

On the day of Rafi's arrival, Nour had accepted Emily's company for a walk on the beach. They made their way around the headland as far as the entrance to a small cave exposed by the low tide. On the way back they followed the water's edge, letting the foam from the breaking waves refresh their bare feet. Nour spoke little, occasionally picking up a pretty pebble for her collection, and Emily relaxed. Lulled by the repeated smack of the waves, she allowed herself to daydream that Rafi kept her company on the sunlit beach.

As they strolled back uphill, she was surprised when Nour shrieked, dropped her small bag of pebbles and raced ahead. She flung herself into the arms of one of the estate workers, who picked her up and swung her around. Bending to retrieve the scattered pebbles, Emily did not immediately realize that the worker was Rafi.

Approaching, she noted the subtle differences between him and his men. Although he wore the same uniform of jeans and an old shirt, he was set apart by an indefinable air of authority. The other workers moved away, leaving Rafi and his daughter together.

He took a step forward when he saw Emily, and offered her an impersonal handshake, as he had done in the hotel. Here, the gesture seemed at odds with his casual attire and bare forearms. Even though he dusted his hand on his jeans, she felt the grains of earth on his smooth, dry skin as his palm touched hers. Her breath quickened at the fleeting contact, sending an uncomfortable flush through her, as if she were still a gauche schoolgirl.

'Hello, Miss Ryan.' Emily's hackles rose, a reaction that owed as much to annoyance at her own awareness of him as to frustration in the face of his self-assurance. How dare he? He must know what his daughter was like. He had sent her to cope with a moody teenager, and here he was, a week later, acting as if nothing was amiss.

'Emilee, her name is Emilee, Papa,' Nour corrected him.

'Yes, please call me Emily.' The words were polite, but she hoped her tone conveyed reserve. The man owed her an explanation and she was going to make sure she got one.

They turned for the house and Emily dropped behind, noticing an ease of movement in Rafi's walk that echoed his ease of manner. She became conscious of her sea-stained skirt and dusty toes and hurried away to freshen up.

Neither Rafi nor Nour, heads together, appeared to notice her departure. *Why should they?* she thought bitterly as she reached the sanctuary of her bedroom. *I'm the hired help, just like Meriam.*

★　★　★

Emily felt better after she had splashed rose-scented water on her face and combed her hair. She opened the shutters that had been closed against the afternoon sun, and pulled her few dresses out of the cupboard.

To feel in command of the situation, she must look her best; but her spirits sank as she examined her meagre wardrobe. Having picked up the habit of travelling light in America, she had packed little to come to Morocco.

There was her old standby, the long, black, wash'n'wear T-shirt dress that rolled into a ball for packing. She held it to the light, wondering how she had ever kidded herself that it looked elegant.

She did have one new dress, a colourful print she had bought in New Orleans. *That won't do either*, she told herself. In Taghar, bare shoulders were taboo beyond the beach.

She held it against herself. *It's too pretty to throw away. Perhaps I could get a jacket or a shrug made. In deep*

31

pink, or else a dark red. The idea made her smile. *This country is getting to me.* A few months ago she would have thrown the dress into the bin and bought a new one. She had bought and discarded so many clothes on her travels. With no regrets. That was life. You moved on, and put mistakes behind you.

If only.

The have-it-all, have-it-now society had sucked her in and the consequences had caught up with her. Yet in Taghar it was impossible not to notice how things were recycled, with nothing useful thrown away. The thought struck her out of the blue: *That's what America was like in the pioneer days.* She took a while to think around that, wondering how long it had taken her own impoverished Irish ancestors to lose the habit of self-reliance once they made it to the land of opportunity.

Her father had certainly lost the habit, if her mother's tirades were to be believed. According to her mother, Emily had inherited all her dad's fecklessness.

She shook off gloomy memories. So what if she had a streak of her father in her? She had been no slouch at running her own life since he abandoned them. Proof of that was that she had got herself here to Taghar. All she needed to do now was sort out exactly what her duties were, and sit tight for a few months while the money rolled in.

She put a clean T-shirt under her new dress, pleased to note that it did not spoil the line. Then she sat down to do her make-up. Natural might do for the beach, neat might do for the village, but only elegant would do for Rafi. Although she was his employee, she would show him she knew her worth.

The final touch was her turquoise-and-lapis-lazuli necklace, its chunky stones set in silver. It had been costly — but, whatever the damage to her credit card, the necklace had not been a mistake. On the contrary, it was always a conversation piece.

And so it proved when she entered the courtyard. Nour's first comment was about the necklace. Even as Emily answered her, she was aware of Rafi's scrutiny and of his slight start of surprise on her entrance.

He pulled out a chair for her. That simple courtesy placed them on an equal footing — host and guest rather than employer and employee. Emily held his eyes for a moment, noting the approbation in them. When he took his own seat opposite her, she was armoured with new poise. Pleased that he had seen her as she wanted to be seen — as a woman.

'Now we can eat,' was all he said. Emily, who had turned to talk to Nour, did not notice that his green eyes lingered on her.

* * *

It was unthinkable to confront Rafi in front of Nour. Despite her annoyance at the casual way he had treated her earlier, Emily vowed to be pleasant during the meal. The admiration she had glimpsed in Rafi's eyes boosted her confidence. *I'll talk to him later.*

As the sky darkened from cobalt to indigo, stars appeared overhead. Meriam placed a yellow, glazed *tagine* pot in the middle of the table, and removed its tent-shaped top to reveal a whole chicken simmered in spices.

Rafi said something in Arabic and turned to Emily. 'I told her that's what a man needs after a hard day's work,' he explained.

Indeed, Meriam was beaming. It struck Emily how Rafi's arrival had cheered not only Nour but his housekeeper too. The frown lines seemed to have vanished from the older woman's face. *She's less grumpy. No, that's wrong; less watchful.* Then she dismissed her reaction as fanciful. What was there to be watchful about in sleepy Taghar? *For goodness sake. Nothing ever happens here.*

The dull gleam of Rafi's wedding ring caught the lamplight as he dipped bread into a dish of sweet peppers. He had changed out of his working clothes into a dark silk shirt, but Emily sensed the farmer beneath the surface. Although his fingernails were scrubbed clean, there was a fresh scratch on the back of his hand.

Capable hands, Emily noted. *Shapely hands*. She shook herself out of her reverie to pay heed to what Rafi was saying.

'What have you been doing to our Emily, my chicken? I can see that she likes it here.' Although he addressed Nour, a smile danced at the corners of his mouth — a smile that encompassed Emily.

The comment riled her, partly because her pulse rate instinctively quickened. Yes, she wanted him to notice her, but not to tell the world. All she needed was a little boost to her confidence to allow her to negotiate a set of rules with him.

She was unsure how to react to his comment. He had pitchforked her into an awkward situation. Now he was patronizing her; she was not *his Emily*. There was no way she would ever be *his*

Emily, and she had mixed feelings about being here.

'I would say that the air of Taghar has put a bloom on her face. Don't you agree?'

Resentment clouded her thoughts. She had no intention of responding to flattery. *He could say that straight out to me, instead of hiding behind his daughter.* She forgot that a moment ago she had wanted him to keep silent.

'Taghar is pretty,' Emily declared, hoping that a curt reply would put a stop to what she decided was a blatant attempt to charm her.

'It's dead. Nothing ever happens here,' Nour complained. 'I want to go to Paris.'

Rafi shot her a quelling look. 'You're too young. Isn't that right, Emily?'

Emily was torn. Rafi might be gone tomorrow, leaving her alone with this grouchy girl. If she wanted to gain Nour's friendship, it was unwise to side with her father on what was obviously a sore point. On the other hand, it was obvious his refusal sprang from concern for his daughter's welfare. Well aware of the dangers to be found in any big city, Emily temporized.

'Taghar is sleepy, but that's its charm.' She was surprised to discover the spell Taghar had cast on her in the few days she had spent there. *Taghar is a safe haven. Whatever happens in the outside world, Taghar will remain inviolate.*

'I've never been to Paris, but if it's anything like London, you might find it overwhelming,' she told Nour. She smiled across at Rafi. Two adults complicit against an eager child.

'Do you miss London?' Rafi inquired. Emily breathed a sigh of relief that the conversation had turned back to a safe topic.

'No.' She noted his look of surprise. 'I don't know. It is my home city. I suppose I'll go back some day.'

'You don't sound sure.'

'It's been a long time since I lived there, and I've been to so many other places since.'

'You could send us both to Paris,

Papa, if Emily has not yet seen it.'

'Paris is out of the question.' Rafi ruffled his daughter's hair to take the sting out of his words. 'Besides, it is not fitting for young women to travel alone. It is not safe.'

Emily seconded him. 'It can be dangerous. But I kept my wits about me.'

Rafi frowned. 'Surely you did not travel alone in America?'

'Of course I did.' Emily dismissed the hint of disapproval in his voice, and explained to Nour: 'America was exciting, but it's all a bit of a blur now. I planned to travel by Greyhound bus, but I soon realized that America is so huge, and took planes instead.' To Rafi, she added, 'Planes are safer, too. You get less hassle.'

He looked unconvinced, his green eyes dark and opaque now in the shadows cast by the oil lamp. For some odd reason her words had disquieted him. She felt uncomfortable under his direct gaze, and plunged on, 'I started in Chicago, where my dad said his folks came from. Then of course I had to do New York. I worked in a skiing hotel in the Rockies over the winter, then I did Vancouver and Seattle in the spring. I took time out to see the Painted Desert and the Grand Canyon. And I ended up working in New Orleans.' Emily drew breath. 'So, you see, London seems a long time ago.'

Rafi did not let the subject drop. 'I was told you had worked in America. I assumed you had been with a family.'

So what? What's that got to do with you? Emily almost said it aloud. She was no teenager innocent in the ways of the world. His censorious reaction puzzled her, for she remembered the admiration she had seen in his eyes earlier. The fleeting but frank admiration of a man for a woman. Surely he knew grown women took their own lives in hand.

Trust Nour to make it worse. 'Papa, you remember I told you she worked in a gift shop. I want to work in a shop when I am older. You get to meet lots of different people.'

'You'll never need a job, my chicken. I'll always be here to look after you.' Nour glared at her father but subsided.

Searching for a neutral topic of conversation, Emily asked Rafi about the work he had been doing that afternoon. And, to her relief, the conversation drifted to general matters.

Rafi made no further comment on her trip. But it seemed to Emily he kept glancing in her direction, as if reappraising the situation. Perturbed, she wondered if her revelations made her an unsuitable companion for his daughter.

★   ★   ★

Meriam returned after clearing the table and sat down uninvited. Rafi rose and returned with an assortment of packets in his hands. Emily sensed Nour almost wriggling with anticipation, and realized this was some kind of ritual.

'Don't be so impatient,' Rafi teased

Nour. 'You'll get yours soon.' He handed the first parcel over to Meriam, who beamed with pleasure as she unwrapped an assortment of dates and fragrant spices. She waddled away to the kitchen, well pleased with her booty.

'Now for your turn.' Rafi placed a small parcel in front of each of them.

Emily was touched, for she had not expected to be included. She smiled back at Rafi — a smile of unfeigned pleasure and gratitude.

'I hope I have chosen the right colour for you, Emily,' Rafi said, as she tore the paper open. 'I thought it would match your eyes.'

His comment went unheard, for Emily sat frozen — staring at a small purse intricately embroidered with blue beads. Nour had one embroidered with silver thread. A child's gift, for both of them. Disappointment flooded Emily. It did not matter what colour it was. She had deceived herself. It had been politeness, not admiration, she saw in his eyes. She had made no impression on him. He saw her as a child still, no older than Nour. No wonder he disapproved of her travelling alone.

'You like it?'

Hurt that he viewed her as a child, she answered, 'It's pretty,' more curtly than she had intended. Looking down at the purse instead of at Rafi, she did not see his puzzled look. 'I'll find a use for it.' Disappointment slid under Emily's skin, an unexpected flat feeling that made her ungracious. She could hear the pettishness in her reply, but found it impossible to sound more enthusiastic.

'It is from a shop in Casablanca that specializes in such work,' Rafi continued. 'Not many tourists find their way there.'

With an effort, Emily remembered he was her employer. She must control her feelings and show gratitude, otherwise her plans for getting her life back on an even keel would be in jeopardy. She raised her eyes and met his across the table. 'Thank you so much,' she said, managing to smile, pleased when his face cleared at her words. His satisfied expression went some way to healing her hurt, and she cast around for something else to say, something more positive. She knew he meant well. 'I didn't expect you to bring me a present. In fact, it's the last thing I expected.' Which was no lie. If only the two gifts had not been the same.

'It is natural. If you live under my roof, you become one of my family,' Rafi declared. 'That is the Arab way.'

At the mention of family, something twisted in Emily. No-one had ever invited her to belong. She had no family that she knew of. Only a worn-out, disillusioned, irritable mother. Setting aside his good looks, there was a core of strength in Rafi. Awareness of inner strength held in check had been part of her initial, instinctive response to him. Now he offered her something else she had never had. Protection and the shelter of his roof. Part of her wanted to believe him. Part of her wanted to cry.

To cover her embarrassment, she homed in on the latter part of his declaration. 'I thought we were in Africa, not Arabia.' Emily would be the first to admit that her notion of geography had always been hazy.

Nour giggled at her ignorance, and Emily was subjected to a history lesson. Hundreds of years ago, the Arabs swept westward across North Africa, Nour explained, intermarrying over generations with the native Berber tribes. She took pride in the history of her people, Emily noted, and Rafi in turn looked on fondly as his daughter took centre-stage.

Nour suddenly became embarrassed at the attention and stopped mid-sentence. She abandoned the table, and returned with a backgammon board and some brass coins in her new purse.

The three of them played backgammon far into the night, alternating partners. When the air in the courtyard cooled, they moved indoors. Emily knew the rules, but she discovered that Rafi had a competitive streak that was lacking in Nour. With only a low table between them, the swift, decisive movements of his lean, brown fingers invaded her space as he moved counters around the board. Against her, Rafi played to win. Impatient when a throw of the dice put her ahead, and triumphant when his luck changed. Against his daughter, he cheated against himself, allowing her to accumulate a little pile of coins on her side of the table.

The open affection between father and daughter pulled Emily in conflicting directions. Painful memories from her childhood surfaced. When playing, she blotted them out by concentrating on her next move. When she sat and watched, her mind roamed and memories nagged at her. She could not remember her harassed, frazzled mother ever sitting down to play a board game with her — not even when she was little. London might be her home city, but if she was honest, she knew it was no longer *home*. Her embittered mother had made that clear when Emily announced her intention of tracking down her absent American dad. *I won't eat humble pie, I won't*, had been Emily's reaction when her mission failed. Instead, she salvaged some pride by throwing herself into exploring America.

On the other hand, Nour's earlier sulks over Paris had vanished in her absorption in the game. *She looks like a twelve-year-old tonight*, Emily thought, watching the girl count her store of coins after every round. *It's the first time I've seen her look happy.* Contentment seeped through the room, enfolding Emily in its embrace. Her first, negative impressions of the job evaporated.

That was Rafi's doing, Emily realized. It was Rafi who brought a sparkle to his daughter's eyes. It was Rafi who included Emily in his gifts to the household, and who invited her to join the backgammon game. Beyond his duty as a host, Rafi had knitted the three of them together.

She had been entranced by Taghar

since her arrival, but felt an outsider in her hesitant exploration of the village. Even the shy waves and greetings she received from the village women emphasized her feeling of otherness. Now, thanks to Rafi, she felt Taghar accepted her.

3

The next day, Emily woke to find Rafi had already left for the orchards. She sipped coffee and contemplated her best course of action. It might be wise to tackle him out in the open, well away from the house. That way, she could be sure of having a private conversation.

She needed to clarify her position. Now that she had seen Nour's likeable side, Emily was impatient to get to know her better — though she was still unsure exactly what role she was supposed to play.

She had no time to waste on her appearance, and did not bother to change into good clothes. It was more important to find Rafi and sort out some ground rules. She pulled a clean shirt over her jeans and set off through the lemon groves.

Although trees blocked the view, she

smelled fragrant woodsmoke, and headed uphill towards it. She followed a track that was barely visible under the dappled shade of the trees, then a broader pathway defined by the wheel ruts scored into its dusty surface. She located the bonfire on a patch of cleared land, where the clean smell of freshly-sawn wood underlay the smoke.

Rafi did not immediately see her, and Emily had her first unguarded view of him at work. His muscles pulled the shirt tight across his shoulders as he bent to pick up sawn-off branches and throw them into the flames. Away from the fire, an older man checked the settings on a chainsaw, his demeanour sullen.

'Emily! I had not thought to see you up here.' A smile lit up Rafi's face when he turned and saw her. He wore his farmer's uniform of jeans and checked shirt, rolled up to reveal bronzed, muscular forearms. The bonfire had left black smuts on his hands and arms. He planted his fork upright in the ground, and came toward her. As he wiped the sweat off his face with the back of his hand, he left a black mark on one cheek.

'I followed the smoke. I guess you're busy.'

'We are. No matter, I am pleased to see you.' His voice rang with genuine pleasure. Emily's heart lifted at his welcome. *I am pleased to see you.* His words echoed in her head, in a surge of excitement that drew her into his world. *He meant it when he called me family.* Then Emily reminded herself about the purse. Rafi was being kind. The way he would be kind to a child.

A log rolled out of the fire in a shower of sparks. Rafi steered her away from the fierce heat. 'You need boots up here.'

'What are you doing?'

'The trees are diseased. The wood is rotten inside.' In one powerful movement, he snapped a slender branch across his knee to show her, and threw the splintered remains onto the fire.

'All this will be cleared. Then I replant.' His gesture encompassed the whole orchard. The older man, noticing the gesture, muttered in obvious disagreement. Rafi made a sharp rejoinder and pointed to the chainsaw. The man picked it up, scowling, and pulled the starter cord.

'Shouldn't he be wearing goggles?' Emily blurted out.

Rafi's air of welcome evaporated. 'Tell me, Miss Ryan,' he inquired with icy politeness, 'do you always meddle in other people's business?'

Emily was furious. She had spoken without thinking, but that was no reason to dismiss her suggestion out of hand. 'If he wears goggles, he'll protect his eyes.'

'I am well aware of that.' He shouted something above the noise of the saw, and the man pulled a battered pair of goggles out of the pocket of his jeans and put them on.

'Satisfied, Miss Ryan?' His voice was frosty. 'Abdullah is one of my oldest workers. He is well able to look after himself.'

Emily felt foolish. She was right, and she knew it. Until Rafi wrongfooted her. Her natural concern for a fellow human being had been twisted against her.

'I thought he didn't have any; I didn't want to see him hurt,' she replied.

'So you jumped to conclusions. We are not savages in this part of the world, Miss Ryan. I take my employees' safety seriously.'

Rafi called out to the old man, who switched off the motor to listen, then cackled. Rafi translated: 'He thanks you for your concern, but says he was cutting down trees before your father was born.'

Emily was convinced Rafi had toned Abdullah's words down. Concern for a fellow human being evaporated when the man leered at her. There was no other word for his expression. As he turned away to move the chainsaw into position, she saw him spit. Humiliation flooded her. Never mind that she had had no chance to talk to Rafi. She wanted out of there.

She fled for the edge of the clearing, but Rafi followed her, catching her elbow to detain her. 'Take no notice of old Abdullah. He was one of my father's oldest friends, and for him, my father's word was law. Now that I am setting improvements in hand, he does not like it.'

'Why do you keep him on?' The words slipped out unbidden. *Me and my big mouth. When will I learn to keep it shut?*

Rafi pulled her around to face him, imprisoning both her wrists in his ash-blackened hands. 'Since you have chosen to interfere in my business for the second time this morning, I shall enlighten you.'

Emily winced at the force of his grip. She attempted to subdue her inner trembling, worried he would feel it in her wrists. 'I only meant . . . '

'Meant what? That I should dismiss

him? Just because he is old and makes no effort to hide what he thinks? You are young, Emily, and you too speak without thinking.'

Emily's cheeks flamed, for his comment hit a nerve. She pulled away from his grip.

'Abdullah is a good worker, and whatever looks he gives me — or you — he will do as I tell him.'

He saw that man leer at me. Mortification froze her to the spot. All her life she had regretted her ready tongue as soon as the words were out of her mouth. In her heart, she knew she deserved Rafi's putdown. Yet his putdown was trivial compared to his complicity in Abdullah's unwanted, raw, masculine appraisal. *He saw that man leer and he said nothing.*

'Abdullah is also the breadwinner for his family.'

'I understand.' Her thoughts in turmoil, she barely heard his words. She could not wait to get away. Why had Rafi not intervened to defend her? In

England or America, she would simply have turned her back on an offensive look, confident in her ability to handle any situation that arose. Here, she was out of her depth.

Here, Rafi was the boss. He could have said something, but chose not to. So much for the protection he had offered her last night!

'No, Emily, you do not understand.' Rafi turned her to face him again, and this time she made no attempt to withdraw. 'If Abdullah works for me, his family becomes my family. My responsibility. And Abdullah has a clever grandson who will go to university in France next year. That will cost much money. So I cannot and will not dismiss Abdullah.

'Well, Miss Ryan,' he inquired after a pause. 'Have you nothing more to say?'

'That is generous of you,' she acknowledged through gritted teeth. This time, his words sunk in, although they surprised her. Eighteen months in America had accustomed her to a casual attitude to hiring and firing. 'Things are different here, I see.'

'That is our way. The Arab way.' Rafi's tone was insistent.

The distressing thought struck her that he might take her lukewarm response for criticism of him and his country. She wanted to tell him she admired his loyalty to his men, but confusion stayed her tongue.

Embarrassment flooded her at the way she had jumped to conclusions. In one way, Rafi's frosty response was justified, although that did not make his comments any easier to hear.

The mention of money reminded her of her own delicate situation. She could only hope his notions of his feudal responsibility included his daughter's companion. She could not afford to lose this job — nor did she want to.

★ ★ ★

Emily attempted to subdue her inner turmoil by climbing almost up to the main road. There, she rested under a pine tree, until her breathing calmed and her limbs stopped trembling. Although outwardly composed, she felt disconsolate, flat and empty. She had expected to find Rafi alone, only to find him in the company of that lecherous old man. Then, instead of protecting her, he had taken the man's side.

When she finally returned to the villa, she went straight to her room. Before anyone remarked on them, she must wash away the black smudges on her sleeves where Rafi had held her wrists. She slid out of her shirt, slowly; reluctant now to erase the memory of his grasp. Remembering how urgently he had gripped her, the thought that Rafi had only detained her because he wanted her to hear his views went some way to consoling her.

Nour sat outside in the shade, helping Meriam with some household sewing. Meriam patted the bench beside her, indicating that Emily should sit, before pulling a voluminous white sheet from the pile on the table.

Emily sipped a refreshing glass of mint tea, idly watching a gardener chop up logs for firewood. For the second time in as many days, she felt that Taghar accepted her, and her despondent mood lifted.

She could not help noticing how attractive Nour was when her face was not set in sulky lines. She shared her father's green eyes and dark, wiry hair; Rafi's face, but not his decisive demeanour. Today, gossiping with Meriam, Nour looked like a carefree twelve-year-old, much as she had done last night.

Emily chided herself for her lack of understanding. Her own problems had blinded her to Nour's needs. The girl was ten years younger than herself, barely more than a child. A motherless child who felt abandoned by her father and who had not yet learned to hide her feelings. No wonder she was sulky.

Emily recalled her own teenage years and her epic battles with her mother. She still found it difficult to forgive her parent for being too proud to explain their chronic financial woes to her. The two of them had been cautiously feeling their way toward a better relationship when she had upset her mother again by leaving for America.

Nour had grown up with a single parent. Perhaps she too did not know the whole picture, and consequently misjudged her father. Rafi was a loving parent, but Emily knew love could also feel oppressive. For once, her inner self advocated caution. *I must tread carefully. Let's all get to know each other first.*

★ ★ ★

Emily went to her own room, and tried writing to her best friend Hannah. After a while, she laid the letter aside. *Hannah won't understand*, she thought, crumpling up the pages and throwing them into a corner. *It's a different world here.* She retrieved the letter, smoothed it out, and re-read it:

I don't know what to make of Mr Hassan. Sometimes he comes across as arrogant and overbearing, yet I admire the way he looks after his people. He calls them his family. He's even got me writing 'his people', not 'his employees'. I tell you, Hannah, when you live here — she crossed out the word 'live' — *when you stay here, you begin to understand the way people act. It's feudal, and I thought that went out hundreds of years ago, but in Taghar it feels right.*

She read on. Had she really written that Rafi's skin was the colour of ripe chestnuts? Her pen must have run away with her. She slammed the door shut on the image of Rafi snapping the dead branch across his knee, his knuckles momentarily white under his dark skin, shoulders taut under the fabric of his shirt. There was no need to tell Hannah about that either.

Although she scored out another couple of sentences, she was still on edge and unable to settle.

Once the references to her enigmatic employer were crossed out, life in Taghar sounded idyllic, like an extended holiday. 'Enjoy,' she could hear Hannah saying in her blunt way.

Hannah would have no patience with her qualms. Emily began the letter again, only to abandon it halfway through. She tore both letters into tiny pieces. Even that failed to ease her mood. After pacing the room in some agitation, she burned the pieces in the wash basin. If Rafi read what she had written about him, she would die of embarrassment.

★ ★ ★

That evening, Nour sent word that she was invited to supper in the village. Although Emily had again dressed with care, she felt unaccountably shy entering the courtyard. She was almost relieved to find Rafi in conversation with Meriam. She wanted to see that flash of admiration in his eyes once more. On the other hand, he was her employer, and Emily could do without romantic complications in her life right now. She was here to earn money.

She sipped her yoghurt drink and waited for them to finish. Once Meriam returned to her kitchen, it was difficult to avoid a sense of shared intimacy as dusk enveloped them both and the square of sky above filled edge-to-edge with stars. It was the first time that she had found herself alone with Rafi since their meeting in Casablanca.

Emily plunged in, too restive to sit and make polite conversation. 'We have to talk about Nour.'

'What do you think of my daughter?' It was phrased as a question, but his indulgent, confident tone showed he expected Emily to praise her. Her edgy mood turned to outright exasperation.

'Perhaps you should ask her what she thinks of me,' she retorted.

'What do you mean?'

'I find it surprising that you imposed my company on her without warning.

You gave her no time to get used to the idea first.'

Rafi frowned. 'I was in Casablanca, and my cousin Sofia told me of her problem with you. Once I had talked with you, I saw a solution for everyone.'

'In what way was I a problem?' Emily disregarded the second part of his speech, homing in on his first, provoking words.

'You came to our country under my cousin Sofia's protection. We could not abandon you.'

Emily acknowledged the justice of this. She did not need Sofia Cherif's protection, but the thought of Rafi the buccaneer commander protecting her from life's storms was strangely alluring. Overlying the allure was irritation that Rafi described her as a *problem*.

'So you thought the ideal solution was to pack me off here. You could hardly expect Nour to welcome a stranger foisted on her.' Her unresolved irritation fed on his cavalier treatment of them both. She nerved herself to tell the truth. 'She doesn't even like me!'

Emily was throwing herself on Rafi's mercy. If he took her at her word, she might find herself on the next plane out.

'That's not what I saw last night.' Rafi appeared untroubled by her admission. 'And I judge by what I see.'

Taken aback by his decisiveness, Emily nonetheless spotted the flaw in his argument. 'But you didn't have time to judge me when we met. You couldn't have. We only spoke for half an hour before you sent me here.'

'I liked what I saw.' Rafi smiled at her obvious surprise. 'Yes, Emily, as soon as I met you, I decided you were the right person for Nour.'

'Oh.' Emily did not know what to make of this. His voice, that silky, alluring voice, was quietly confident. There was no teasing note. There was no trace of the edge of impudence that had fascinated her in Casablanca.

He means it.

Emily tried in vain to recall what she

had said to win his approval. 'Why?'

'Nour is of an age to need a woman's guidance. My wife was French. She would have taken Nour to France by now, to — how do you say — to flap her wings.'

Bewildered by his logic, Emily endeavoured to set her thoughts in order. 'But I'm not French.'

Rafi waved that objection aside. 'You are European. You will think like Marie-Jeanne.'

Emily gulped. She had seen for herself the gap between England and America. The gap between England and France must be just as big, but Rafi had casually bracketed both countries together. For a moment, she wondered if he had ever left his own country.

She decided he must at least have visited France, his late wife's country. It was the first time he had mentioned her. Emily took it as a sign he trusted her.

'Tell me about your wife.' She was curious to know what kind of woman had turned the tables on this roguish buccaneer and captured his heart.

'Marie-Jeanne?' Rafi's voice softened, as it did when he spoke of Nour. 'She had a different upbringing.' He looked down at his ring for a moment, then directly at Emily. 'Here in Morocco, what happens to one happens to all. When I make a decision, I decide what is best for everyone. Europeans have no patience with our ways. They focus on what is right for them as individuals, and they act on that. She went at life like a little bulldozer, my Marie-Jeanne. I used to tell her not to run me over, too.'

It was hardly a compliment to the dead woman, but Emily sensed his sincerity. *Rafi must love her still.* Only a man in love could infuse the word *bulldozer* with patent admiration and affection. She liked him for it.

At the same time, it painted a vivid picture of their marriage, one which made her smile. So his wife had stood up to him. It was difficult to imagine the Rafi Hassan she had so far seen giving ground to anyone — let alone a woman.

Rafi had bracketed her with his wife. Emily's self-image did not allow her to see herself as a 'little bulldozer'. Instead, she saw herself as a hard worker. As someone who did not let adversity get her down. Although, she had to confess, she often took decisions without thinking them through.

Emily squared her shoulders and did her best to put on a confident front. Never mind whether she was English or French. If she was to make the most of her opportunities here in Taghar, it was time to sort out her role. 'You want me to be like a big sister to Nour. Is that it?'

'Yes. Keep her company. Talk to her. There is only so much a father can do.'

So there was a chink in his confident armour. Admitting his limits made him more of a man, Emily decided.

Rafi judged his daughter by her happy face when he was present. He would not like what she was going to say. However, he ought to know what Nour was like when he was absent.

'Nour resents me.' She saw Rafi's start of surprise. How best to explain it to him? 'It's you she wants. It's you she misses. I'm a poor substitute for you.'

Emily saw he was unconvinced. Inspiration came as she recalled the cosy evening the three of them had spent together. 'We could have a day out together. The three of us. If Nour sees that you approve of me, she might come round.'

And I will see more of you.

To her relief, Rafi agreed. 'Good idea. We will arrange something soon.' He suggested possible outings, and Emily, knowing nothing of the countryside beyond Taghar, agreed to them all.

There was no easy way to move on to the next question, but Emily had to ask. She had burned to know the answer since she met him. 'How long is it since . . . How long have you two been alone together?'

'My wife died five years ago. Nour has been at school since then. When she came back, I could see how much she had changed.'

His words brought Emily up short. 'What school? Where?'

'In Agadir. It is our nearest city.'

'A boarding school?' That explained the absence of older children in the village, something which had puzzled Emily.

She sensed him stiffen and heard the shock in his voice. 'We do not treat our children so. Nour lived in the household of my brother and sister-in-law.'

He could have told me that before. She looked back over the past week and realized how hard she had to work at dragging conversation out of an unco-operative Nour. *And I thought I was getting to know her,* she reflected ruefully.

'And you wanted her home again?'

Rafi hesitated. 'I have asked Meriam to complete her education by instructing her in the kitchen.'

Emily hid a smile at his quaint attitude. She had never heard learning to cook described as 'completing an education'. 'Didn't your sister-in-law do that?'

'My sister-in-law is a modern woman. She told me homework came first while Nour was at school.'

She heard the hint of reservation in his voice. 'Don't you agree with that? I do.'

'My daughter did well at school.' There was pride in his voice. 'But book learning is not everything, Emily.'

At that moment, Meriam brought in a platter of stuffed peppers surrounded by black olives. Emily thanked her.

Rafi, seeing his point made, dipped his bread into the spicy sauce. As he licked his fingers clean, his eyes challenged her to disagree.

Although not a word was said, a kaleidoscope shattered and reformed in Emily's mind. She forgot Nour. Her lips parted as she stared at the slow, sensuous movement of Rafi's fingers.

Time stood still. Was his gesture deliberate? She could not say. The previous evening, he had appeared to be no more than a courteous, attentive host, with a hint of admiration in his eyes. Emily was used to attracting male admiration. It was something she could handle. Tonight, grappling with her shattered preconceptions, she did not know how to react. She sensed her shallow, erratic breathing.

'Do you still say that homework is more important?' Although his eyes gleamed with mischief, the words brought her down to earth. *What was I thinking of?*

'Not when I taste Meriam's cooking,' she conceded, licking her own fingers clean in unconscious imitation of his gesture. She prayed her crazy thoughts had not shown on her face.

The peppers were replaced by a dish of sweet fritters sprinkled with almond flakes. Rafi bit into one, offering the other half to Emily with a murmur of appreciation. The tips of his fingers felt sticky against hers. Yet his words were factual and kept her at a distance. 'Meriam makes these with special honey from the Atlas Mountains. We have a cousin who has a farm there.'

Although she murmured her appreciation in turn, Emily could not have said what the fritter tasted of. Only the fleeting touch of his fingers remained.

She pressed her own fingers to her temples to clear her thoughts. 'Did you have another reason to bring Nour back here?' she probed, aware that something else lay behind his earlier, uncharacteristic hesitation in replying.

'Emily, you have good sense. You put your finger on my problem.' It was the first time he had complimented her. Certain now there had been no ulterior motive behind Rafi's earlier actions, she stored the words away to treasure later. It was her job to concentrate on his worries as a father.

'Agadir is a big city.'

That figures, she reflected, remembering his overprotective reactions the previous evening. 'As big as Casablanca?'

She had been struck by the contrast between the bustling modern city she had glimpsed on arrival, and the sleepy tradition that ruled in Taghar. Centuries separated the two.

'Nowhere near, but there are bad influences in any city.'

The trigger for Nour's return had been the fact that Rafi's sister-in-law allowed Nour to attend a daytime disco — with boys invited. It sounded sweet and innocent to Emily.

Yet Emily had seen for herself how Nour's eagerness for her father's company made her seem younger than her years. No wonder Rafi thought of her as a baby still.

She lived away from home, Emily reminded herself. It was another reason for Rafi to remember the child she had been.

'I agree with your sister-in-law. Girls going to their first disco are more interested in dressing up than in meeting boys.'

Rafi's face reflected his doubts.

Emily persevered. 'You said yourself your wife would have taken her to France by now. I understand that. At sixteen or seventeen, all young girls want to try out their wings.'

'In her mother's company, visiting her mother's family, I would have no worries. If Marie-Jeanne were alive, I would leave the decision in her hands.'

He appeared lost in thought for a few moments. 'It is not that simple. Change comes to Morocco. Our children face a different future. If I had a son — a son to follow in my footsteps — I would know how to talk to him.' He grimaced. 'I lack a woman's touch to talk to my daughter.' Abruptly, he asked, 'Would your parents have permitted such a party?'

'At seventeen, my mother would certainly have let me go.'

'And your father?'

'He wasn't around.' She stiffened on hearing Rafi's instinctive snort of disapproval. 'My mother brought me up. My father left home when I was twelve.'

'That is not good.' His tone was harsh, uncompromising.

The bruise on Emily's heart had never healed, but it hurt to hear Rafi criticize her father.

'I've never condemned him out of hand. He must have had reasons — reasons I didn't know about.' Fitful happy memories of her father were warped by her mother's repeated rants.

'There can be no reason for a man to abandon his family.'

Emily heard the finality in his voice. His comment stung, as any criticism of her father hurt. She blinked back her tears. From what she could see, Rafi Hassan went to the other extreme. He sought to protect his daughter by locking her in a golden cage. Who was he to criticize her father?

She was saved from the need to answer by Nour's return, full of chatter about her supper invitation. *How pretty she looks tonight.* She wondered whether the evening had given her the opportunity for a stolen chat with one of the local boys.

You'll learn, Mr Rafi Hassan. You can't wrap your daughter up in cotton wool forever. No father can.

* * *

As the almond trees shed their blossom, carpeting the terraces beneath them, the household fell into a routine. Although Rafi made regular trips to the factory in Agadir, he usually returned for the night. It seemed to Emily he had taken to heart her concerns about Nour missing him.

Rafi left early for the orchards, and returned for the midday meal. He ate in his workman's uniform, and his conversation centred on the estate. At suppertime he metamorphosed into a courteous host, setting Emily at her ease with small talk.

At first, it unsettled her that Rafi never crossed the line into flirting with her. It was not that he was unaware of her. Several times she noticed him glancing at her with appreciation — and not just appreciation of her looks. As her backgammon skills improved and she won her first games from him, his eyes danced with enthusiasm at the challenge he faced.

Over the weeks, Emily relaxed her guard. Soon, she felt no shyness in his company. Apart from those discombobulating instances when their surroundings melted away and she became suddenly aware of nothing but his closeness. In those moments, it was as if a protective layer of skin had vanished, leaving all her nerve endings jangling and awaiting his touch.

Rafi did not mention the proposed outing again. Emily did not press the matter. For one thing, the estate and the business kept him busy. For another, she no longer needed an excuse to be in his company.

Most mornings, Emily and Nour walked down to the bakery. It was the only shop in the village. They watched fishing boats being dragged out of the water by tractor, and took parcels of fresh fish back to Meriam. Nour taught Emily a few French and Arabic phrases, which Emily practised on the shy, smiling village women.

She also practised them on Rafi, much to his amusement. '*Le dernier pain,*' she announced one day, as they returned to find Rafi chatting to Meriam in the kitchen.

'I hope not,' Rafi teased her, his eyes crinkling. 'How will we eat if the baker closes down?'

'It was the last loaf left in the shop today. That's what I wanted to say,' Emily explained with mock dignity.

'Then I'd better have some before it disappears.' Rafi broke a piece off and nibbled on it. Meriam scolded him sharply, removed the vandalized loaf from his reach, and covered it with a cloth.

Rafi winked at Emily. 'She always tells me off.'

'Tell me what she just said.' Emily paused before adding, 'In case I need to tell you off, too.'

Nour supplied the answer, sticking her tongue out at her father as she did so. '*Ne sois pas gourmand*. In English, that means 'don't be greedy'.'

Rafi held up his hands in mock surrender and backed away. 'I have no chance in a house full of women.'

As she watched him leave, Emily filed away the phrase about being greedy. Rafi was a hearty eater when he had been working outdoors. She looked forward to seeing his face when she used it on him.

Most afternoons, once the heat of the day abated, Emily and Nour paid a call on one of the village women, or on Nour's aunties. Afterwards they went for a lazy swim, followed by a walk along the shoreline looking for pebbles. Nour often threw stones back on the beach, claiming to have found prettier specimens, and Emily had a hunch that the pebble collection was no more than a much-needed excuse to escape Meriam's prying eyes.

It was the evenings Emily cherished.

Although the villa was spacious, its rooms were furnished in a simple, almost Spartan style, with cedarwood chairs and tables. To Emily, it felt homely.

On evenings when Nour was invited elsewhere, Rafi lingered with Emily in the courtyard after the meal, the fragrant smell of his cheroot rising toward the square of brilliant stars. When Rafi was invited elsewhere, Nour was reticent and voluble in turn. She often quizzed Emily about the antics of American pop stars in the magazines she read. This made Emily aware how out of touch with teenage tastes she had become.

Rafi might set limits to his daughter's freedom, but under his own roof he was an indulgent father. Over their shared suppers, Nour chattered freely, as if his presence bolstered her confidence.

One such evening, it occurred to Emily that there was no reason to adhere to her self-imposed six-month deadline. She was well paid, and Taghar had embraced her. Despite Nour's bouts of reticence when Rafi was not there, Emily felt closer to the naïve, eager girl who thrived in her father's presence.

Admittedly, Nour seemed young for her age. Emily vowed she would work on Rafi to allow her more freedom. His indulgent, protective words echoed in her mind. He talked of sending her to France later to 'flap her wings'. From a Western perspective, Emily believed what Nour needed was space to unfurl her wings right here, right now.

Given Rafi's stubbornness, that might take some time.

4

A few days later, a car drove up to the gates, and Rafi introduced the young driver to Emily: 'My assistant, Nassim Mansour.'

'*Enchanté.*' Nassim shook her hand, holding it for a fraction longer than was necessary. After a brief acknowledgment to Nour, he followed Rafi into the house.

Creep, Emily judged. *I've met his type before.* However, the two men closeted themselves in Rafi's office, and she thought no more about him as she lazed the afternoon away on the beach.

Nassim stayed for the evening meal and was invited to stay the night. Emily could have done without his company. His presence blighted the comfortable atmosphere that had developed between the three of them. Several times he paid Emily an extravagant compliment. She bristled. *As if he expects me to simper back. He's years younger than me!* In any other context, she would have told him to get lost, in no uncertain terms. At her employer's table, she had to smooth matters over and hope Nassim got the message. She could only hope Rafi did not think she welcomed Nassim's flowery speeches.

The men vanished after the meal, as did Nour. But Emily was too restless to go to her room and sleep, and decided to go for a walk instead. She had not ventured outside late at night since her arrival, but was sure there could be no danger. *This is Taghar*, she told herself, slipping out of the main gate.

She had not walked far when she sensed movement to her left. She hesitated, and was relieved to make out a couple in a passionate embrace under a tree. As Emily stepped back, they emerged onto the road. By the light of the stars she could see Nour and Nassim.

'Emily, Emily!' Nour ran to catch her

up. 'You must say nothing,' she pleaded.

Mistaking agitation for embarrassment, Emily apologized. 'I'm sorry I disturbed you. I had no idea Nassim was your boyfriend.'

Fingers dug painfully into Emily's arm. 'You must not tell.'

'Why not?'

'Promise!' Nour's voice rose in panic.

To avoid a scene, Emily agreed. She returned to the house, needing time to think. Nour was seventeen, and she felt a sense of responsibility toward her. *I'm paid to look after her.* On the other hand, this might also be the breakthrough that would allow her to gain Nour's confidence.

Rafi entrusted her to me. I won't let him down. If she could encourage Nour to open up and talk to her, she would be in a better position to mediate between father and daughter.

Emily splashed rose-scented water on her face and looked at her reflection in the mirror. *Since when has it become so important not to let Rafi down?* she wondered. Rafi Hassan expected life to go his way. Why should Emily care if his daughter rebelled against him? *He should have expected this*, she decided, suppressing the uneasy voice that told her otherwise.

In fact, the more Emily thought about it, the less she liked the situation. Nassim looked no more than twenty, but that was old enough to know he should discourage a teenage girl's infatuation.

There was another reason to dislike him. *Nassim flirted with me to divert Rafi's attention*.

Although the hour was late, Nour came to repeat her plea for secrecy. Emily reluctantly promised, but resolved to keep a close eye on the girl in future. In an isolated village, that should not be too difficult.

'Why won't your father like it?' she probed. 'Nassim is his assistant. Obviously your father trusts him.'

Nour shook her head in denial. Emily cudgelled her brains. *What would*

Nour's mother have said?

'Let me speak to him for you.' Yes, that was what a mother would do.

The offer agitated the girl still more. 'No-one must know.'

'Why not?'

'I am expected to marry my cousin Tariq.'

Emily sat down on her bed in shock. 'Who's Tariq? And why must you marry him when you . . . you like Nassim?' Emily bit back the word *love*. Love was an adult emotion, and she wanted to avoid planting the word in Nour's mind. 'Calm down. I won't say anything. Tell me what's going on.'

Clearly, Nassim's facile charm had turned the girl's head. *We all make mistakes*, Emily told herself. *It's part of growing up*. At the same time, there was an eager, trusting side to Nour, and Emily did not want to see her hurt.

Nour plumped down beside her. 'Ever since I was born, I am told I must marry Tariq.'

'What!'

'The marriage was arranged between my grandfather and my new grandmother.'

'This is the twenty-first century!' Emily exclaimed. 'Women are not chattels.'

With the air of a teacher expounding the two-times-table, Nour explained, 'My grandfather married again. And my new grandmother already had a son, my cousin Tariq.'

'So he's not really your cousin?'

'Have I not just told you? He is my new grandmother's son. And when my grandfather died, he left some land to my new grandmother, knowing she will marry Tariq to me and the land will come back to our family.'

Emily gulped. 'Do you agree to that?'

Nour looked puzzled by the question. 'It is expected of me.'

'But if he's your grandmother's son, isn't he a lot older than you?'

Nour's laughter pealed out. 'Tariq is three years younger than me. He is a stupid baby still.' Seeing Emily's confusion, she explained, 'My new grandmother is younger than my father. She is very beautiful and everybody likes her. So now she lives in Agadir where everybody invites her to parties.'

That cleared up one question in Emily's mind. 'But what if you don't like Tariq? What then?' she persevered.

'If Tariq grows up to be a bad man, then Papa would never make me marry him.' She shocked Emily by adding, 'Meriam says I should not expect too much from a husband. That way, I will not be disappointed.' Nour looked untroubled at the prospect.

Emily was dumbstruck. She had heard of arranged marriages, but had never dreamed a loving father like Rafi would guide his daughter toward one. At the same time, she remembered the clipped tone of his voice when he had told his daughter that Paris was out of the question. Not only did Rafi Hassan live in the past where his daughter was concerned, but he did not like to have his decisions challenged.

'What about Nassim?' Emily so

wished she had not made that promise. Out on the road, in the dark, she had not stopped to think. *Nassim must know about this Tariq. And it hasn't prevented him seeing her in secret. This is wrong.* She must find a diplomatic way of breaking her word. Not yet, though. Not when she had just given her promise.

The girl's face was animated. 'Nassim is handsome, don't you think?'

'Yes, but should you be kissing him if you are going to marry this other man? I mean, boy. What would Tariq say?'

'*Bof!*' Nour dismissed Emily's comment. 'Tariq is not here to see. But you understand why you must say nothing. To nobody.'

* * *

The next day Emily heard from Meriam that a beach picnic had been arranged. Meriam sent her to buy extra bread after breakfast. On her return, Emily was surprised to find heaps of vegetables and fresh fish on the table. '*Pique-nique*,' Meriam explained, indicating the piles. Emily recognized the word, despite the foreign pronunciation.

Meriam took a pan of dry-roasted spices off the stove, and tipped them into a small, stone bowl, crushing them with a blunt pestle. Emily sniffed as the spices released a tantalizing aroma, but she could not identify any individual flavours. She poured herself a cup of coffee and sat to keep the housekeeper company. Meriam appeared jumpy again, glancing toward the open door as if expecting a visitor — although Emily had seen nothing amiss in the village. It puzzled her.

They made their way down to the beach in the late afternoon. The two plump aunties were already there. 'They've picked our favourite spot,' Nour whispered to Emily, before joining in a chasing game with the younger children.

Emily sat with the women as Rafi and the men hunted for stones to build the barbecue and set the fire going. Out of politeness, she accepted a gooey sweet-meat from one of the aunties, although she did not want to spoil her appetite for the coming meal. Meriam had bustled around all morning, and Emily was sure the offerings would be as delicious as the smells that wafted through the kitchen.

Before the meal, she found herself drawn into an impromptu ball game. Unsure of the rules, or whether there were any rules at all, she decided the best thing was to keep an eye on Nassim, who was the leader of her team. That was her downfall. As she ran to catch the ball heading her way, she tripped and fell right into Rafi's arms.

Emily was the more shocked of the two. It had been the briefest of contacts. Rafi seized both her arms and set her on her feet again. '*Hop-la!*' was all he said. From the way the others smiled, Emily knew it meant no more than *oops*.

Heart pounding, she could not rid her senses of the hard feel of Rafi's chest as he caught her. They had both been fully clothed, which made no difference. Even through his shirt, she had felt the muscles quiver, and had smelled the lingering, citrusy fragrance of his cologne.

Wanting to stroke her own arms at the spot where his hands had gripped them, she disciplined herself not to do so. She made her excuses and left the game to sit down beside the aunties.

Emily turned her face to the setting sun and pulled her beach hat down to protect herself from its rays. She needed time to compose herself.

Back in Casablanca, she had been tempted to fall for Rafi's impudent charm. She was glad now that circumstances had conspired to make that impossible. A fleeting affair would tarnish them both.

What she felt today was totally different. In Rafi's arms, for a brief moment, she had felt safe. Safe for the first time in her life.

Surprise knocked her sideways. Safety

was an alien feeling. Emily had relied on herself since she was a teenager. She had never expected to need anyone else in her life, let alone a man. Men were unreliable.

The traitorous tingling, that had started at the spot where Rafi's bare hands had gripped her, invaded her whole body. But her physical response was nothing beside the memory of that delicious feeling of safety.

* * *

Rafi watched her go. He could not follow her. That might cause gossip. Even he knew how the village women loved to gossip, embellishing insignificant events in the retelling. He had a particular responsibility toward Emily, as a guest in his country and a guest in his home. Gossip might be a fact of life in Taghar, but he intended to shield her from it.

He had witnessed her confusion when she stumbled against him. That was another reason for not following her out of the game. He did not want to add to her embarrassment.

To think he had only met her in Casablanca as a favour to Sofia! Sofia had asked him to explain the situation in person, out of courtesy to a foreigner. He had come with a pocketful of notes, prepared to pay her off and send her back home. Until he met her face to face.

The Emily he had seen in Casablanca had something about her. Something indefinable that recalled the days of his youth, when life lay in front of him with endless possibilities. Something that made him change his mind.

Tonight, Rafi congratulated himself yet again on his decision. Emily had been a breath of fresh air for his daughter. She brought the outside world with her.

Taking skilful aim, Rafi kicked the ball close to the water. The children rushed to rescue it before the waves reached it. He held up his hands to the others in apology, satisfied that he had distracted attention from Emily's sudden departure.

He would join her later, he decided. By then, she would have recovered from foolish embarrassment over her stumble.

★ ★ ★

As the sun sank into the Atlantic breakers, the picnic party demolished the last bites. Emily sat silent, without feeling obliged to join in the chatter around her. By now, she had learned a few words of French and Arabic, but Taghar accepted her as she was.

Watching Nassim and Nour, she had to admit they were being careful. They had moved away from the group and were walking along the water's edge, silhouetted against the blood-red sun. However, a small child walked between them. The child grabbed their hands and they began to swing him off his feet.

Rafi came to sit beside her, his gaze

following the two young people, but Emily saw no sign of wariness in his face. Instead, she thought she detected approval.

Emily endeavoured to concentrate on what he was saying. It was difficult even to sit there and listen to the man when her body quivered in response to his presence. With an effort, she dragged her attention back to what he was actually saying.

'It is good to see my daughter enjoying herself.'

Emily found herself unable to answer. On the one hand, the knowledge of Nour's secret rendered her tongue-tied. On the other, she attempted to ignore the sensations that danced through her veins. *I must say something sensible.* If she kept Rafi talking, it would take her mind off his unsettling physical closeness.

'I wish her mother could see her now.'

The mention of his late wife brought Emily down to earth. There was no escaping the knowledge that Rafi had once shared plans and dreams with his wife.

On the other hand, Rafi's words presented her with an unexpected solution to her dilemma. A trip abroad would extricate Nour from Nassim's clutches without any need for her father to know. *It's just what she needs.*

'Why not send Nour to her mother's family in France?' she asked. 'For a short break to say hello.'

Rafi made a face. 'Not without her mother.'

Nour's mother. His wife. His late wife. Yesterday, she would have welcomed Rafi speaking of Marie-Jeanne as an indication of his friendship. Now, she wanted to brush her away as an irrelevance. He was a free man, and he was sitting close to her. His legs stretched out on the sand inches from hers. Awareness of his physical presence almost robbed her of the power of speech.

Emily swallowed. Nour spoke now and then of her mother, but Emily had the impression she was a distant memory in the girl's life. Clearly that would not apply to Rafi, who still wore her ring.

'What part of France did your wife come from?' Emily asked, feeling her way. She tried to keep the conversation factual, and allow her own desires no chance to surface.

'From the north. It is a small village, much like this one.'

That answered one question in Emily's mind. 'But if it's a quiet village, I can't see any problem. Not if she's visiting her mother's family.'

'Perhaps next year. She is young yet.'

That's what you think, her inner voice commented. She was the only one who could push Rafi toward a solution, she realized. She must convince him sending Nour to France was his own idea.

'Nour is old enough to know what she likes and dislikes,' she began. Her heart lurched under her ribs, reminding her that she too had fallen prey to ungovernable yearning. She shut the door on that, and plunged on. 'It is difficult for her without friends of her own age. The other children in the village are much too young. A trip to France would broaden her horizons.'

'So she keeps telling me.'

'I thought it was Paris she had set her heart on. And I agree with you on that. A big city isn't the best place to start exploring a new country.' Emily cudgelled her brain to think of other arguments to nudge him in the right direction.

Rafi, however, was thinking along other lines. 'The trouble is, I have indulged my daughter too much. Now she thinks she only has to ask and I will give her whatever she wants.'

Emily looked at him in surprise. It was not the impression Rafi had given so far. If his strict rules were no more than a reaction against fond lenience in former years, maybe persuading him to give Nour some space might be easier than she thought. It was on the tip of her tongue to share her worries about Nassim with him. *Not now. Not yet.*

'When she was little, I would have

given her the sun, the moon and the stars.'

'Naturally. All fathers feel that way.' Emily said it lightly, but his words sent a stab of desolation through her. Her own father was a distant memory. She so wanted to believe that he too would have given his little girl the sun, the moon and the stars. Instead, he had walked out on her and her mother. Emily had learned early that men could not be trusted.

The unhealed hurt of long ago threatened to overwhelm her. All because she heard a man speak lovingly of his daughter. *Get a grip*, she told herself. With an effort of will, she concentrated on the last sliver of blood-red sun as it slipped out of sight.

Her breathing slowed. She was back in control. The heightened awareness of Rafi's closeness had gone too, which made it easier to talk.

She persevered with the task of persuading Rafi, feeling she owed that much to Nour. 'I've never been to France. I don't know what it's like. But I do know Nour is chafing at the bit here.'

'The bit? I do not understand the word.'

'It means a horse is eager to start running.' She saw Rafi shake his head in bewilderment. 'I meant that she wants to see the world beyond the village. And it's not just that she wants to, she needs to.'

Rafi's eyes narrowed. His quick brain focused on her last words. 'Needs to?'

Emily drew a deep breath. He needed to hear the truth from her and not discover it by other means. *Then what happens to me? I'll have to leave Taghar and never see Rafi again.* Duty warred with desire.

Duty won. 'Nour is seventeen,' she said crisply. 'You need to trust her more. Let her see the world. It's a normal part of growing up.'

Rafi stood up to bury the stub of his cheroot in the sand. 'That is precisely why I invited you here. Instead of sending my daughter out into the world, I am bringing the world to her. Here where she is safe. Here where I am in charge.'

*　*　*

Emily slept badly. She was unable to subdue the merry-go-round in her head. Awake before dawn the next day, she splashed her face with rose-scented water from the enamel bowl. She sat on the edge of the bed, trying to disentangle her conflicting thoughts.

Yes, she wanted Rafi; but afterwards . . . what then?

The picnic had brought to a head the attraction that had been simmering unresolved since she had met him. The attraction she had tried so hard to suppress. She had thought she had herself under control. Until the startling moment she felt protected in his arms. *Where do we go from here?*

Unable to supply a satisfactory answer to her own question, she slipped out of the silent villa. In the faint glimmer that heralded dawn, she followed the road as it zigzagged up the hillside between the grassy terraces. Occasionally she smelled the distinctive fragrance of an isolated pine.

Sitting on a boulder, she rested. After a while, she kicked her sandals off and rubbed her bare feet on the short, springy grass. The chill from the dew shocked her fully awake, but she was no closer to a solution in her own mind.

It will have to be the whole package. Am I ready for that? She was unsure. Rafi was too honourable to offer her an affair. In his world, it would be marriage or nothing. *Is that what I really want?* For the hundredth time she asked herself the question. She reviewed the glimpses she had gained of his sense of family and duty. Could she live up to his exacting standards?

The whole package would include his daughter. Emily was growing to like the girl, but did that mean Nour would welcome her as a stepmother? Emily's muscles tensed against possible rejection.

Then there was Rafi himself. He had

been businesslike toward her in Casablanca, with an edge of devil-may-care charm. Despite the admiration she sometimes glimpsed in his eyes, since then he had shown her nothing but courtesy and respect.

How to take matters further? How to persuade Rafi to open up? There were no easy answers.

The first call to prayer of the day sounded from the minaret, startling her out of her reverie. The confusion Emily had felt since leaving the villa vanished as she heard the soothing, ageless rhythm of the calls that punctuated life in Taghar. Rafi's life.

Her friends sometimes told her that she believed what she wanted to believe. In candid moments, Emily had to admit that was true. Not today, though. Today, at last, she knew her own mind.

But when the call to prayer ended and she rose to go, uncertainty returned. Wanting Rafi was one thing: getting what she wanted, another.

Walking back downhill, trying to put

her thoughts in order, she paused for a good look at Rafi's village and the ocean beyond. The waves had begun to shimmer in the sun. There was a speck of movement in the water. She saw a small, military-looking boat travelling at speed away from the headland. On the flat rooftops, sleeping figures roused themselves. The villa, too, would be waking up. She would see Rafi at the breakfast table. She quickened her pace.

★ ★ ★

Her reflections might have been different had she known Rafi had also woken early, his thoughts monopolized by the startling memory of catching Emily in his arms. Night had brought the realization that he wanted to hold her — to reassure her — to banish that alarmed, embarrassed look from her face. He was sure now that her independence was a front. Emily needed looking after.

In Casablanca, he had not foreseen this complication. What to do? His head told him to pay her off and send her back to her own country, where she had a mother to look after her. He would find another companion for Nour.

His heart told him to keep Emily close, here in Taghar. But here he was her employer, and that meant he must not take advantage of her.

For Rafi, too, duty warred with desire.

5

The next day, they followed Nassim's car north along the road to Agadir. Emily sensed Nour's eagerness. The younger girl sparkled with unfeigned, childlike enthusiasm. More than ever, Emily was convinced that all Nour needed was space to make her own mistakes.

Meriam came with them, sharing the back seat with Emily while Nour prattled away to her father in the front. When Rafi halted the car next to some market stalls, Meriam extracted her bulk from the back seat, and shook open what Emily had taken for a rolled-up umbrella. She transformed it into a voluminous, chequered holdall.

'*Au revoir*,' Nour called after her.

'*Au revoir*,' Emily echoed, but Meriam stumped off.

The car turned off the main street and drove through an area of factories and warehouses. Heat blanketed the town, and the stubby palm trees by the road-side offered little shade.

'Here we are,' Nour exclaimed. 'This is Papa's factory.'

'What do you make here?'

'Pottery,' Rafi answered. 'It's good business,' he said, embracing the building and car park with an expansive sweep of his hands. 'Nour will show you around,' he added. 'Later we will show you Agadir, but for now I have business to attend to.'

'This way.' Nour pulled at her hand and led her to the showroom. Brightly decorated cups and dishes lined the display shelves.

Emily exclaimed in surprise. Meriam used the same pottery back at the villa, but the effect of a massed display was striking. 'Everything is so pretty! I must buy a coffee set for my mother. She'll love the colours.'

Nour smiled. 'All here is for export. My father has an office in Belgium.'

'Why Belgium? I'm sure you could

sell this stuff anywhere.'

Nour shrugged. 'We have cousin in Antwerp.'

I should have guessed. Cousin was an elastic word in Morocco, covering any sort of family connection. Everyone Emily met had been introduced either as a cousin or a dependent, and she suspected Morocco was one vast web of inter-related families. 'And Nassim, is he your cousin too?'

Nour looked flustered. 'He is university graduate. He understands modern business. My father is sometimes old-fashioned.'

She needn't be so embarrassed about her father, Emily thought. Judging by the size of the premises, the business was a successful one. And it was Rafi who had created it, not Nassim. She changed the subject by asking Nour where she could send an email.

After checking her bank account, Emily wrote to Hannah. Startled to find that her words came out as gibberish on the screen, she looked down and realized the keyboard layout was different. She started again, taking care to put her fingers on the correct keys. Her frustrations ebbed away as she wrote. *This will amuse Hannah*, she thought, as she made a cheerful tale of her efforts to learn a few words of Arabic and the misunderstandings she walked into on her daily trips to the village.

Something stopped her pressing 'Send'. As she re-read the email, she realized she had revealed more than she meant to, and she was using an office computer. Was it wise to confide her impressions of village life to a communal workstation?

Again, she had written too much about Rafi. She flushed to read words that betrayed her deep admiration.

He takes a real interest in people in the village. The way he looks after them is remarkable. Not just money, but he always seems to think about what is best for them, what will suit their circumstances.

What Rafi promised, in his crisp,

confident way, he delivered. Emily suddenly wished she could hear Rafi promise to take care of her. If only he would say those very words in his silky voice, she would fall into the safety net of that promise.

She read on:

When I first met him, I thought he was unbelievably sexy and gorgeous. He's from the south, where they have skin as tanned as copper and black, crinkly hair. I wanted to reach out and feel his hair curl around my fingers. Now I don't even notice what he looks like. If I had my eyes closed I would still know when he came into the room. I would recognize his voice. I think I would feel his presence even if I were blindfolded.

Her finger hovered over the 'Delete' key. Then she changed her mind and left it all in. Let Hannah mock. She would burst if she did not tell someone how Rafi made her feel.

There were contradictory sides to Rafi. She had tried to describe them all.

There was the confident businessman, and the farmer who got his hands dirty. There was the loving father, and the man trapped in feudal tradition, who exaggerated the danger to his daughter beyond the confines of his own village.

What if he reads this and sacks me? Robust common sense came to the rescue and told her not to be so ridiculous. *Someone else might read it, though, and I have been indiscreet.*

Hannah was her main link with the outside world. *What if he doesn't let me use the computer again?* It was a wretched thought, making her all too aware how isolated she was in this foreign land. She deleted the entire letter, angry with herself for doing so, and sent Hannah a short, non-committal email.

★ ★ ★

An uncharacteristically silent Rafi collected them for lunch. Emily was surprised by the contrast between the featureless, dusty industrial zone and the spacious seafront. As in Casablanca, she stepped back into the modern world, with hotels that would not look out of place on the beachfront of any large city. Rafi, however, guided them to the terrace of a smaller, more traditional establishment.

The terrace was crowded with families and felt cool, with a light wind coming off the ocean. Their small group blended in and Emily did not feel conspicuous as she did in Taghar. A few foreign tourists were identifiable by their guidebooks and cameras. People were minding their own business and taking little notice of their neighbours. *Just like home*, she thought.

She studied the other family groups, beguiled by the exotic blend of lifestyles on view. Schoolgirls in skinny jeans who flaunted designer sunglasses on bare heads shared tables with women who wore sturdy headscarves over their traditional, shapeless *djellabas*. She was intrigued by the diversity of skin colour, marvelling at faces that ranged from dusky peach to dark caramel, a legacy of mingled

Berber, Arab, African, Spanish and Portuguese bloodlines.

Emily shook her head over her silly imaginings in the factory. She was not isolated in an alien land. Morocco was a melting pot of tradition and modernity. Taghar might be remote, but the throbbing pulse of modern city life was never far away.

Hannah would have that chatty email as soon as possible, she resolved. She could ask to use the computer again that same afternoon.

'Do you come to Agadir often?' she asked.

'Not often enough,' Nour complained.

'Don't start,' Rafi snapped.

He gave no answer to Emily's question and seemed lost in thought. Emily wondered why his mood had changed since the morning. Perhaps the factory was not as successful as it appeared to be. *Businesses are on a knife edge all over the world*, she reasoned.

'Rafi!' Emily was startled to hear a female voice calling. A stylish woman threaded her way between the tables. She came to a stop in front of them, embraced a reluctant Nour and leaned across the table to brush Rafi's hand with her fingers. Emily, she ignored.

Her exclamation had made people turn to look. Emily acknowledged the new-comer would not go unnoticed anywhere in the world. Her clothing was a subtle fusion of European and local styles, and a gauzy scarf revealed rather than con-cealed artfully highlighted curls.

As she drew back her hand, and sat down uninvited, Emily could not suppress a twinge of envy at the sight of perfectly-lacquered scarlet nails and a profusion of gold bangles around slim brown wrists. She thrust her own unmanicured hands deep into her pockets and clenched her fists.

'I thought I might find you here,' the newcomer purred. 'There is a small matter of business I must consult you on. Would you have an hour to spare for me this afternoon?'

'I regret, Samira, I have obligations

today.' His gesture encompassed Nour and Emily.

Samira looked at her for the first time. 'Who is this?'

'Emily. She lives with us now,' Nour volunteered.

'I remember. You are Sofia's nurse-maid.' Before Emily could muster a reply, she lost interest and turned back to Rafi. 'No longer than one hour, I assure you. For your cousin, you can do this one little favour. I am a woman alone in the world, as well you know. I am in need of a man's guidance.'

Like hell you are, thought Emily, already irritated by the woman's discourtesy and prepared to think the worst of her. She was annoyed to see that the stranger's blatant approach had an effect on Rafi.

'When you put it like that . . . ' He shrugged and summoned a waiter. 'Here.' He passed a handful of notes to Nour. 'Take Emily to the *souk*, while I have a word with your cousin.'

'I thought we were going back to the factory,' Nour protested.

Rafi ruffled his daughter's hair. 'The factory is business, my chicken, you would only be bored. Business is better left to grown-ups, is it not, Samira?'

Samira produced some more notes and pressed them on Nour.

Emily picked up her bag and stood up. She could not wait to get away from the table. Anything was better than sitting there watching Rafi endorse the woman's commands.

She could not resist a backward glance. Samira's hand was on Rafi's arm, and she leaned across the table as she talked. Emily was flooded with unaccustomed jealousy.

'Did you want to see Nassim again this afternoon?' she asked Nour, as they left the hotel and the doorman hailed a taxi for them. 'Is that why you wanted to go back?' Her own plans for emailing Hannah had been foiled, and she did not know when she would find another opportunity.

'She is cow!' Nour burst out. 'Did you hear what she said to me? '*Buy yourself some sweets.'* She thinks I am five years old still. When Papa marries her, I will drown myself in the sea.'

The mention of marriage hit Emily like a physical blow, knocking the breath out of her. 'It's not polite to call someone a cow,' she reproved Nour, hoping her voice did not tremble. How could she have overlooked the possibility that Rafi might have developed an interest elsewhere in the years since his wife's death?

'She is poison!' Nour hissed. 'Do you prefer me to say that? It is the truth,' she continued. 'When her husband died, she decided to marry my father. She will eat him up like a crocodile. But he does not see that.'

Nour complained bitterly about her cousin during the short taxi ride. Emily, stunned, made no effort to stop her.

However, the *souk* was so entrancing that she forgot about Rafi and Samira. The alleyways were crammed with tiny, open-fronted stalls selling carpets, pottery, perfumes, beaten copper jewellery. She had no chance to linger, for Nour pulled her along, tugging at her sleeve whenever she stopped to look.

'Come, I show you good shop.' They found the one she was looking for. Nour paused for a quick, respectful greeting to the shopkeeper before lifting the curtain at the rear.

Emily relaxed when a young girl came downstairs in answer to Nour's call. They disappeared together for a few minutes, then Nour returned, her face cheerful. She steered Emily through the maze of lanes at a slower pace this time.

'Here,' she announced. 'This is best shop for fabric. You choose one, and I will return in five minutes.' She was gone before Emily could object.

At first she filled in the time admiring the bolts of shimmering fabric. To her embarrassment she found that every time she touched one, the owner pulled it down and spread it over the counter for her to inspect.

'Please, no, I wait for my friend,' she tried to explain.

'Wait, yes, I understand.' To Emily's

further embarrassment, the owner cleared a chair for her and sent a small boy to fetch a glass of mint tea. Emily sipped the tea slowly, hoping Nour would return soon.

In the end, she decided she could not sit there without buying something. She looked at the fabrics again, and decided on a length of embroidered blue cotton. She would have a local tailor make her a *djellaba*. They looked cool to wear in the heat.

Disaster struck when Meriam walked past the open-fronted shop just as the assistant was wrapping Emily's purchase. She spotted Emily and directed a stream of sharp questions at the shopkeeper, who shrugged his shoulders.

I could wring that girl's neck, Emily thought, uncomfortably aware of Meriam's accusing stare. It had been a good twenty minutes since Nour had disappeared, and it took her another ten minutes to arrive back at the fabric shop. Nour's shock when she saw Meriam standing guard over Emily was more eloquent than words.

Rafi sat alone on the terrace when they returned. One look at Meriam's angry face and Nour's tearful one was enough. Meriam unleashed a flood of explanations. Rafi motioned to Emily to sit, while Meriam marched Nour inside.

'Well?' His voice was cold.

'Well, what? We got separated in the *souk*, that's all.'

To her Western ears, it sounded reasonable. She had made that rash promise not to betray Nour, but she was not going to shoulder the blame for misunderstandings.

'I pay you to look after my daughter,' Rafi said, emphasizing each word. To her dismay, his lean, chiselled face was hard and set. The camaraderie he had shown her at the beach barbecue vanished. What had that Samira woman called her? *Sofia's nursemaid*. The words rang in Emily's ears. Yesterday, Rafi had spoken to her as a friend. Today, under Samira's influence, his tone was impersonal, an employer reprimanding an employee. More than his words, the tone wounded her.

'If I leave her in your charge, it is your job to look after my daughter, and my daughter alone. You do not disappear to look at what interests you.'

Stung by the injustice of his accusation, Emily did not pause to consider that worry might underpin his anger. All she saw was his flinty expression. *You didn't say anything about us staying together. Once that woman appeared, you just wanted to get rid of us.*

She derived satisfaction from putting the worst possible interpretation on his actions, although she knew in her heart her criticism was unwarranted. Rafi was strict where his daughter was concerned, but he was fair.

Emily, you have good sense. She had cherished those words since Rafi first said them in his low, silky voice. She repeated them to herself now. Surely he could not imagine she had lingered half an hour in the fabric shop by choice.

'I don't speak the language. I didn't

know what was happening.'

'You appeared to have no difficulty in making the shopkeeper understand you.' His voice was as flinty as his eyes.

'I had to buy something,' she retorted hotly. 'I was there so long, it was only polite.'

'Precisely! You spent a long time shopping for yourself, without making any attempt to find my daughter. If you had not neglected your duty, there would be no need for your so-called politeness. Your job is to accompany my daughter at all times.'

The unfair accusation took her breath away. 'She vanished. What else could I do?'

'She is young, and thoughtless. She went to see a friend whose father has a shop there, and she forgot the time.'

'But — ' Emily bit her tongue. Nour had seen her friend before she left Emily. The only explanation was that Nour had somehow contrived a meeting with Nassim. Perhaps the other girl had lent her a mobile phone. That was it! If all she wanted was a girly chat she could have left Emily downstairs in the first shop.

'But what?' Rafi seized on her words.

It was impossible to say anything to clear her name. Not without betraying Nour. Now was not the moment for that. She cast around desperately for an alternative explanation that would satisfy him.

'Girls forget the time when they're chatting. What's so bad about that?'

Rafi frowned. 'It was a harmless escapade, but she should beware of gossip.'

'Why should anyone gossip when they were safe upstairs in her father's shop?'

Mistake, she realized too late. He would know she had been in the shop. *I'm not cut out to be a double agent*, Emily agonized, angry with Rafi for making deception necessary.

Rafi appeared not to notice her slip of the tongue. 'It is not what happened, it is what *might* happen that matters.'

'Nothing *did* happen!' Emily salved her conscience by telling herself there had been no time for more than a couple of stolen kisses. What Nour needed, in Emily's mind, was to mix freely with boys her own age. That would cure her of her infatuation with the unctuous Nassim. 'You and Meriam are making a mountain out of a molehill.'

She had burned her boats, but his inflexible attitude angered her. Let him dismiss her if he wanted to.

Instead, Rafi replied with quiet civility. 'In this country, we respect our women. We protect their honour.'

'Nour is not a woman yet,' Emily replied hotly. 'You said yourself, she's still a child. It was a misunderstanding, that's all.'

The grim set of his mouth relaxed. 'I know that, you know that,' he conceded. 'But the world does not know that, and I will not have people gossiping about my daughter. I have her reputation to consider.'

'Her reputation will hardly suffer because she had a chat with a school friend in the middle of the afternoon,' Emily observed tartly. Although she was on dangerous ground, she was determined to press her point.

Her reasoning had no effect. Rafi maintained his flinty civility, a civility that held Emily at arm's length. 'Emily, you know nothing of our country and our way of life. My daughter's reputation must be spotless. It is my job as her father to shield Nour from danger — and gossip — until such time as I find her a suitable husband.'

He spoke with such honesty, Emily caught her breath, her resentment deflected. If only her own father had taken his paternal duties as seriously as Rafi. Which was worse, she wondered; the over-protective Arab way, or her American father's flight from responsibility?

Rafi gave a sudden chuckle, surprising Emily, who was still smarting from his homily. 'Believe me, Emily, I do not envy her future husband. I love my daughter, but I have indulged her too often.'

'You cannot be thinking of marriage already.'

'Not for many years. She is a child

still, with a child's understanding of the world.' He shrugged. 'Today, she did not think. I will tell her so.'

Emily remembered Nour's tearful face as Meriam hustled her into the hotel, and had no doubt that the girl would receive a double reprimand. If Nour had not landed her in such trouble, she might have felt sorry for her.

'You do not know my daughter like I do,' Rafi told Emily, spreading his hands in a gesture of resignation. His annoyance had evaporated but his tone remained grave. 'And you are new to our ways. I warn you now, this must never happen again. Agadir is not Taghar. Taghar is our home. And in Taghar, there is Meriam, who has known my daughter since she was born. In the city, you must be watchful at all times.'

He rose, and Emily followed him.

* * *

In contrast to the happy atmosphere of the morning, the drive home was uncomfortable for everyone. In the front seat, Nour sulked beside Rafi. No-one said a word to Emily, who sat squashed in beside Meriam's bulky shopping bag.

Matters did not improve over the next couple of days. Nour avoided her. Cross with the girl for putting her in an awkward position, Emily nevertheless told her that her secret was still safe. Instead of thanking her, Nour scowled and flounced away. More than ever, Emily was convinced the best way forward was to allow Nour the freedom to make new friends of both sexes. *She'll grow out of him*, Emily assured herself, disregarding the small voice which told her otherwise.

Rafi's endeavours to mend fences with his daughter in the evenings were equally rejected.

'How about a game of backgammon, my chicken?'

'Not with you. Not when you treat me like a stupid baby and let me win.' Nour slouched into the sofa, and flicked over the pages of her magazine.

'How do I get her to talk to me?' he asked Emily later.

The bewildered look in his eyes cut her to the heart. She considered telling him about Nassim. As Nour's father, he had a right to know. *Then he'll realize she ran away to meet him in the* souk. Emily panicked, remembering his fierce reaction. She could never tell Rafi now. If he was angry then, how much angrier would he be when he discovered they had both deceived him?

'Give her time.' The lame answer satisfied neither of them. They talked around the issue, but guilt stopped Emily's usual candour. It was not a pleasant feeling.

★   ★   ★

The frosty atmosphere in the villa gave her a chance to take solitary walks and reflect on her position.

Rafi was going to marry Samira — his elegant, sophisticated cousin.

I was mistaken. I believed what I wanted to believe. Her dreams had been just that — dreams. There was no future for her and Rafi.

The uneasy feeling that she had indeed let him down only heightened her sense of grievance. His daughter was seventeen, not seven. He could not expect Emily to hold her hand every time they set foot outside the gate.

Worse was the sense of loss. Loss of the warm cocoon of welcome she had found in Taghar. Rafi's curt tone when he reprimanded her rang in her ears still. The memory of his chilly politeness mocked her futile hopes for the future.

In the heat of the argument with Rafi, she had also forgotten her debts. Life in Taghar, in the slow lane, encouraged her to forget them. Alone on the beach, she reminded herself how much she owed. Another reason to curb her ready tongue.

Restless and miserable, Emily eventually decided to track down Nour for an English lesson. She desperately wanted a reason to stay on in Taghar, close to Rafi, and English lessons justified her presence. She found Nour playing with a kitten under the almond trees and dropped to her knees beside them, glad of the shade. But Nour was uncommunicative, and after a few minutes Emily abandoned her efforts at conversation. In an exasperated mood, she lay back and closed her eyes.

Her doze was interrupted by Meriam. Emily propped herself up on her elbows and wondered what was happening. Whatever it was, it seemed to have brought the feud between Nour and Meriam to an end. They muttered angrily, but in concert, not in opposition.

As they moved away, Emily called after them. Nour ran back and stood before her, her face flushed with anger. She spat the words out. 'Samira, she come to stay with my aunties.'

6

Emily and Nour were lingering over bowls of yoghurt with rose-petal jam when Samira walked in early the next morning. Emily had grown accustomed to the way the village women walked into the courtyard unannounced when looking for Meriam or Nour, but that was usually later in the day. Even Meriam looked flustered by Samira's early arrival, for she appeared almost immediately. Emily had not yet forgiven Meriam for reporting the incident in the *souk* to Rafi. *Spying on everyone; doesn't she have anything else to do?*

Watching Samira as she sat down, Emily marvelled at her ability to look elegant. Although Emily had dressed carefully that morning, hoping to catch a glimpse of Rafi before he left for the terraces, Samira's very presence made her feel gauche and gawky.

Samira ordered coffee for herself. Nour pushed back her chair, and announced that she was going for a walk. Samira, however, caught her sleeve before she could escape. 'Don't run away, my poppet.'

There was a sulky expression on Nour's face as she sat down again, but Samira took no notice.

She turned to Emily. 'You may take the morning off, Elsa.'

'My name is Emily.'

Samira waved the remark away. 'My cousin and I have a lot to talk about, haven't we, darling? You are growing up, and it is time we renewed our acquaintance.' She patted Nour's arm. 'I expect Meriam can find you something to do,' she added in Emily's direction.

Nour stayed silent and Emily carried her coffee cup back to the kitchen, wishing that she could smash it onto the stone floor to ease her frustration. It was not Samira's deliberate rudeness, although that was bad enough. It was her air of effortless elegance that riled Emily.

She took herself out of the house,

walking down to the baker's on a totally unnecessary errand. Here and there, she kicked a stone away from the path, experiencing a perverse pleasure as the dust coated her clean sandals again.

I can't compete with that. Nobody could. She looks as if she's stepped straight out of Vogue.

She was still looking down at her sandals, feeling inadequate, when she met Rafi coming up the path.

'Oh, you startled me!' she exclaimed.

'No wonder. You were lost in your thoughts. Tell me, what troubles you?'

Emily stared at him wordlessly. She hardly heard the question. The sun was on his face, and she could focus on nothing else. For once, his face was on a level with hers, since he stood below her on the path. She was aware of a sudden longing to stroke his copper skin, to reach up and trace his lean features, from his temples around to that single earring, along the jaw and around to his mouth. To brush his mouth with her fingers. She took an involuntary step backwards to escape the compulsion.

'Emily, are you all right?' There was concern in his voice.

'Yes. Sorry. I was thinking, that's all.'

He raised his eyebrows.

'It's nothing, it's not important.' She was babbling and knew it. 'I'm on my way to the bread shop.'

'Allow me to accompany you.' The polite request disguised a command.

'You needn't, really, I'm sure you're busy.'

He turned, and fell into step with her. 'Do you not want my company?'

The reply was torn from her. 'Of course I do.' She wanted his company, not just for a ten-minute walk, but for every minute in the day, every day. Walking beside him was a form of torture, one she wished would continue.

It seemed her wish would be granted, for when they arrived at the bakery, Rafi took her elbow to steer her past it.

'You can buy bread on the way back. Let's take a turn on the beach.' He paused before continuing. 'What is wrong, Emily?

Today your face is sad.'

Seeing the genuine care in his eyes, Emily did not trust herself to speak.

'Well, Emily?' Rafi questioned. 'You, who are so ready to give your opinion, have nothing to tell me today?'

'No.' Her voice came out as a sniff.

The concern in his face deepened, and she knew her reaction was childish. It was up to her to accept his approach in the spirit in which it was given, to control her feelings and enjoy his companionship when it was offered. Companionship was not what she wanted; every taut fibre of her body told her otherwise. But it seemed that for now she had no choice in the matter.

They walked in silence for a while. Their feet crunched on the shingle. When they reached a sandy stretch, Emily took off her sandals. While she did so, Rafi moved ahead, searching for stones to throw far out into the waves. He became absorbed in this pointless task, not even looking at Emily as she stood on the water's edge, allowing ripples of foam to caress her bare toes.

She felt deflated. The day had seemed so full of promise when Rafi had invited her to walk with him. She had pushed him away, but she was upset to see him ignoring her. As if sensing her pettish mood, a cloud passed briefly across the sun. Close to tears, Emily stared out to sea, pretending to focus on a container ship on the far horizon. *Let him turn round. Right now, when I'm not looking in his direction. Let him see I don't care.*

Emily resisted the temptation to turn herself. Rafi was to marry Samira. Nour had told her so. She dared not reveal any sign of her own attraction to him. Instead, she stood on the very edge of the waves, eyes half-closed against the salt-laden breeze. Each retreating wave sucked a little more sand from under her feet. As she stepped back to regain her balance, she noticed a small blue pebble glistening on the wet sand. Attracted by the unusual colour, she picked it up. The surface was pitted, the colour dark but translucent. A shard of glass tumbled smooth by the waves.

Like me. Cast onto a Moroccan beach by accident. Like the warrior Vandals who had invaded North Africa in ancient times and been expelled again, leaving as their legacy a sprinkling of green eyes among the native Berber tribes. *When Rafi marries Samira, I'll get thrown back in again. Then where will life take me?*

Lost in her thoughts, Emily failed to notice the approach of an oversized wave until it smashed onto the shore, soaking her up to her knees. She stepped hastily back and let her skirt hang down to her ankles again, feeling the wet hem stick to her legs. It would soon dry in the heat, but it was her best skirt, the one she had worn to impress Rafi should he happen to see her at breakfast. If she wanted to wear it again tonight, she would have to wash it.

She risked a sideways look at him, but by now he was in conversation with one of the villagers. *I might as well walk back. He won't even notice I've gone.*

However, as she turned to go, one of the village women waved and patted the blanket beside her. Emily hesitated. It was bad manners to snub her. She folded herself down onto the blanket, and smiled hello.

As her skirt dried, she relaxed and eased herself into a comfortable position. She exhausted her few words of French and Arabic, and the rhythmic crash of the waves took the place of conversation. She endeavoured to think rationally. *Where else could I sit on a beach and get paid for it?*

She gave herself a silent pep talk. *Let them get married. I'll go somewhere else, find another job. I survived before, I'll survive again.*

Fool, her heart told her. This time she would not find it so easy to move on.

She felt in her pocket to show her companion the piece of sea glass she had found. She would keep it as a talisman, a reminder of the seductive enchantment of Taghar.

Suddenly, Rafi was there, standing over her, a flesh and blood Rafi who was far more disturbing than the figure she had attempted to banish from her thoughts. She ceased to be aware of the curve of the beach, or the pounding waves. Her neighbour on the rug might have been a million miles away. The world shrank to a patch of sand in front of her, and the man standing on it.

'What's that you've got there?'

Emily was grateful for the commonplace remark. It brought her back to reality.

'Glass, I think. I noticed it because of the colour.'

Rafi scrutinized it. 'From a bottle thrown overboard, I would say.' As he handed it back, he quipped, 'Even on a beach, you find blue. It is truly your colour.'

His comment set Emily's back up. She would not rise to the bait of superficial compliments. After ignoring her for the last half hour, he had no business strolling back without any sort of apology. In her current contrary mood, she refused to acknowledge that she herself was at fault.

'I'll keep it as a souvenir,' she announced, slipping it in her pocket.

Rafi now began a conversation in Arabic with her companion. *Is he doing this deliberately?* Emily wondered.

She stood up. 'I'm going,' she interrupted. By their faces, she knew she had committed a social faux pas. Time was never important in Taghar. There was always time for one more glass of mint tea, one more conversation. Her annoyance focused on Rafi, not on herself. He was the one who had insisted she accompany him. He was the one taking his time.

Her impetuous mood found a welcome physical outlet as she stamped back toward the houses, crunching the shingle underfoot. She heard Rafi's footsteps behind her and tried to quicken her own, but his long strides allowed him to overtake her with ease.

'You dropped this,' he said curtly, showing her the sea glass cupped in his hand. 'If you can't look after it, I will.'

Through her sleeve, Emily felt the spot where he had laid his fingers. Her cheeks flamed. She fumbled for a convincing explanation for her sudden departure.

'I came down to buy extra bread. I'm sure Meriam needs me back.'

'Meriam will need you, not Nour,' he noted. 'It seems that you are avoiding my daughter now, as well as avoiding me.' He planted himself in front of her, blocking her escape, his face grave. 'What happened, Emily? Have you two quarrelled? Is that why you're upset?'

'No.'

'I do not like to see you unhappy.' He waited for her answer. 'Well? Do not deny it.'

Emily wanted to scream. He had backed her into a corner, and she was unable to give a truthful answer. 'Nour is talking to her Auntie Samira. I thought they needed some time together.' It gave her a fleeting moment of satisfaction to describe Samira as an auntie, not a cousin.

For all her sleek facade, Emily guessed that Samira would not see forty again.

Rafi frowned. 'I don't see why you felt obliged to leave. As you know, my daughter can be tiresome. I would have thought that Samira would welcome an ally in dealing with her.'

Trust a man not to see what is staring him in the face. Emily swallowed her temper with difficulty. Samira's earlier brusque dismissal of her still rankled.

'That still does not explain why you left us so suddenly just now. I asked Nadia, but she did not understand either.'

'You two were having a private conversation. You didn't need me there.' *I come last in the queue. After Samira, after Nadia. After the baker too, I expect.*

Rafi frowned. 'I spoke in a language she understood, just as I speak to you in your own language. Nadia is the wife of one of my workmen, and she is also a cousin of my late uncle's wife. It was only good manners to exchange a few words with her.'

Emily could hardly object to that.

She knew Rafi took a genuine interest in his employees' welfare. Today, however, Emily felt ill-used, and was disinclined to give Rafi credit for anything. Samira had been cutting. Then Rafi had ignored her. They deserved each other.

She did not want Rafi to ignore her. She wanted him to look at her and forget the rest of the world — including Samira — the way she had forgotten the rest of the world when he stood over her on the path.

'In Europe, we leave people alone. We give them privacy.' She spat the words out.

Rafi's astonished look jolted Emily out of her bout of self-pity. 'Are you saying I should have left you alone earlier this morning, when I saw you coming down the hill? I disagree. You must learn to accept help when it is offered, Emily. If I see you upset, then I take you for a walk and I talk to you.'

Emily knew she had gone too far. She hastened to make amends. 'I didn't mean to be rude. Apologize to Nadia, please, next time you see her.'

Emily privately resolved to apologize in person, later on. Like the other inhabitants of Taghar, Nadia had embraced Emily with open-hearted Moroccan friendliness. It was not her fault Samira was patronizing.

'I do try to fit in,' she explained to Rafi. 'But I find it confusing when you act like one great big family. Sometimes it's overwhelming. At home we stand back and give each other space.' It was not quite the truth, but it saved a lot of embarrassing explanations.

They had reached the bakery and Emily dived inside, grateful for the diversion. She waited a moment before leaving, to compose herself. Rafi shot her a keen glance as she came out. Constraint lay between them as they walked back up the hill.

Then Rafi removed the warm loaf from her nerveless hands and broke two small pieces off. 'This was one of my pleasures as a small boy,' he remarked, offering one of the pieces to Emily. A

146

smile hovered at the corners of his mouth. 'My mother scolded me when I got home, but she knew I could never resist.' He smiled at the memory. 'Sometimes she told me she had to order an extra loaf, just for me.'

Emily took his words for a peace offering and wagged her finger at him: 'Give it back, or Meriam will scold us both.' As she rewrapped the flat loaf in its square of coarse paper, she remembered the phrase for being greedy. '*Ne sois pas gourmand*, that's what she'll say.'

'Correct. And your accent is improving.'

They began to talk of other things. When they reached the gate, Emily held out her hand. 'May I have that little piece of glass back, please?'

Rafi patted his pockets. He shrugged. 'It seems to have fallen out. I'm sure you'll find another.'

The trivial loss put the seal on a bad morning for Emily.

★   ★   ★

Relieved to see no sign of Samira and Nour, she took the loaf to the kitchen. When she handed it over, Meriam set a cup of coffee on the work table, indicating her wish for Emily's company.

Emily accepted and sipped the pungent brew. When Samira became mistress of the villa, there would be changes. Samira might want to sack Meriam.

Rafi will never allow that. His words echoed in her mind: *If you live under my roof, you are my responsibility.* His patriarchal attitude was infuriating; but, in fairness, Emily acknowledged that Samira was unlikely to rule the roost. Rafi would never allow her to sack Meriam.

Even so, Emily could well imagine that Samira would depress any form of familiarity on the part of a servant, and Emily did not envy Meriam her future role. In a wave of fellow-feeling, she offered to help.

Meriam removed the couscous that

had been steaming over a pan of bubbling stew and tipped it onto a dish. Emily had often seen Meriam separating and massaging the half-cooked grain with oil before returning it to the pan for further steaming. She had never done the job herself, but set to with a will. It took far longer than she expected, but the task proved restful. The hot, wet grain slithered between her fingers as she kneaded the clumps out of it, again and again and again. To her surprise, her mood lifted as she did so. Since it was impossible for her and Meriam to have a proper conversation, they worked in comfortable silence, broken only by the chattering of birds in the trees.

At last the older woman was satisfied, and took the dish from her before pouring them both another cup of coffee. Emily licked her fingers clean of the tangy, peppery olive oil pressed from the estate's own trees.

★　★　★

Her relaxed mood carried her through until the evening. When she discovered that Samira would not be joining them for the meal, her spirits soared. She found the meal companionable, until Rafi started teasing her on her newly-acquired cookery skills.

'Emily, you will impress your husband if you set a couscous like this before him.' He licked his fingers to emphasize his point.

Emily stiffened as Nour commented, 'Perhaps you will marry a Moroccan, Emily, and live here forever. You will have to make couscous every week then.'

The innocent remark was a hammer blow, forcing her to confront her innermost desires. *There is nothing I want more.*

Rafi mistook her reaction. 'I think not, Nour. Emily has no patience with our Moroccan ways. She told me so this morning.'

The way he twisted their conversation on the beach made Emily gasp. 'That's not true!'

'You told me Morocco was confusing.'

His words put Emily in a quandary. Now was not the moment to explain the disappointment that lay behind her pettish reaction that morning. Certainly it was not her place to openly criticize Samira. 'I only meant that sometimes Moroccan hospitality is overwhelming. You're so generous, and friendly, and welcoming. All of you.' *Except for one person.*

'I am pleased to hear it. I would not like to think that we treated you badly.'

'You don't. I mean, nobody has. I mean I like being here.' She shot a quick glance at Rafi, relieved to see his expression relax.

'I will ask Meriam to look for a good husband for you. Meriam knows everybody's business.' That was Nour's enthusiastic contribution, which made the other two smile.

'Not so fast, my chicken. Emily is a modern woman. She will make up her own mind.'

151

Samira's arrival in the village spelled the end of cosy evenings for the three of them. Emily felt bereft. Little by little, those shared evenings had woven a spell around her. They provided her with a haven where she felt increasingly at home. She had even learned how to play chess — after a fashion, for neither of her opponents took the game too seriously.

The only consolation was that, since Samira's arrival, Rafi spent more time at the factory, frequently staying away for a few days at a time. Emily could not be sure if this was by accident or design. He seemed preoccupied, and Emily wondered if the business was in some kind of trouble. It was a pity that he never spoke to Nour about it, for she stood to inherit one day.

Does he really want to marry Samira? Emily's senses were alive to every nuance that passed between the two. Rafi treated his cousin with unfailing courtesy. However, Emily noticed that he rarely teased her as he teased herself and Nour. His eyes never lit up when Samira arrived. Bare courtesy seemed to her an odd basis for married life. Then again, from Nour she had learned that marriage in Morocco was often based on land and family connections.

When Samira shared their evening meal, Rafi went out of his way to include Emily in the conversation. Emily was grateful, for Samira did her best to monopolize him.

'I forget, you do not speak our language,' Samira would purr in her direction whenever Rafi reminded her she had begun to talk in Arabic.

'Emily is our guest, Samira. We must speak so she understands.'

Emily hugged his words to her like a protective cloak and smiled her thanks at him.

Samira's apologies usually had a sting in the tail. 'You must forgive me, darling Emily; my cousin and I know each other so well, when we talk I forget we are among strangers.'

Although Emily was grateful to Rafi for his pointed interventions, Samira's possessiveness toward Rafi set her teeth on edge. The words *my cousin and I* recurred in Samira's conversation. Emily forced herself to smile back when she heard them, refusing to let her upset show.

*   *   *

One day Rafi returned from a trip to Agadir, bearing gifts for all the household. Emily was delighted he chose an evening when Samira was absent. Once Meriam had returned to her kitchen, it was just the three of them, like before.

Nour received silver earrings.

Emily unwrapped her packet. She stared spellbound at the object in her hand.

It was her piece of ocean-tumbled sea glass, set now in a silver pendant. She stroked the pendant, exploring the contrast between smooth metal and pitted glass. To Emily, it was a more precious gift than a diamond.

'Thank you. Thank you so much,' she stammered, overcome by emotion. 'I like it, I really like it. It's unique.'

'It was my idea,' Nour said proudly. 'I told Papa my friend's mother has a necklace made with glass from the sea.'

Rafi beamed. 'Nour and I have long wanted to find something special for you. Then you yourself showed me the way, when you found this on the beach.'

His words made her forget Samira. She was only dimly aware of Nour's chatter. She heard genuine affection in his voice. It almost broke her heart to know that he would never offer her more than that.

She managed to speak. 'I felt quite let down when you said you had lost it.'

'I could see you were disappointed. But we could not tell what we planned to do.'

'Of course not. That would have spoilt the surprise.' Blinking back tears, she gazed at the other two, who looked pleased with the success of their idea.

The pendant was not a gift from a lover. It was a gift from two friends, and all the more precious for that. She clipped it around her neck, and vowed to wear it close to her heart forever.

★ ★ ★

Officially, Samira was visiting the village to attend her cousin Mourad's wedding. Mourad, one of the younger estate workers, was to marry Asmaa. Emily gave up on understanding how many generations ago the cousinship between Rafi and Mourad had originated. It seemed to her as remote as Samira's connection with them both.

The wedding proved a welcome distraction. Emily had not realized that the festivities would last several days, and she became caught up in the general excitement. She waved at the women who scurried between houses with trays of food. She stood at the roadside and waved as trucks and cars came down the hill, hooting extravagantly to announce the arrival of a few more migrant workers travelling home for the long party. Walking past the café on the way back from the beach, she could not help noticing how the new arrivals displayed a defiant sophistication by consuming bottled beer under the disapproving looks of the older tea-drinkers.

The night before the wedding was the bride's henna evening. Dressed in a heavy, embroidered robe and headdress, Asmaa sat on a sofa where all could admire her. Two women stained her hands with rust-red henna, covering palms and fingers with intricate motifs. They painted the guests' hands with simpler designs.

Emily's fair skin and red hair attracted comment when it came to her turn. She was showing off the design on her hands to her neighbours when a murmur ran through the room.

'Eat, eat,' someone urged her, as a plate of honey cakes was passed around. Emily exclaimed in dismay as she bit on something hard. She broke the sweetmeat open to reveal a small silver coin.

The women clustered round, chattering, seizing her hands and pointing to the henna motif. She was pulled upright, still holding the coin.

'You marry,' someone told her in English.

It was not until Nour was summoned from another room that Emily understood.

'It is our custom here in Taghar,' Nour explained. 'The woman who finds the coin will marry before the henna leaves her hands.'

Emily had not realized henna did not wash off. She was submerged with light-hearted suggestions as to which young man she should choose, with the promise that she could inspect them all the next day.

She laid the silver coin under her pillow that night. *It doesn't mean anything, it's just a fun custom.* Yet in the morning, she felt under the pillow to make sure that the coin was still there.

* * *

Rafi danced with her on the day of the wedding, when men and women finally came together under one roof. Emily was surprised at her own popularity. One young man after another drew her into the circle of dancers. Even old Abdullah, almost unrecognizable in a clean *djellaba*, performed a few steps alongside her before his grandson took his place. Emily did not know any of the steps, but held hands and stamped her feet in time to the drumming. From the corner of her eye, she noted that Samira danced rarely, but sat in a corner drinking tea with a group of older women. The sight lent a spring to her step.

She had barely sat down again before Rafi crossed the room to her and led her onto the dance floor. 'I can see you're enjoying yourself. I have not had a chance to speak to you yet.'

'At least I can talk to you.' She gladly took her place in the circle beside Rafi. The day had been enjoyable. She felt at ease with herself and with him. 'I can only speak a few words to the others, but I haven't sat down since the dancing started.'

'You know why, don't you?'

'I found the coin in the cake. Yes, they explained yesterday. But I don't understand. Everyone acts like it's a huge joke.'

'Has anyone shown you disrespect?' Rafi asked sharply.

Emily shook her head. 'Not at all. Everyone is friendly, but it's like I've got two heads. I can feel them all talking about me.'

'Two heads? Nonsense. A man would have to be blind not to notice that you are a beautiful woman, Emily.'

Emily's heart turned over. She forgot to concentrate on the dance. Caught off-balance, she would have stumbled, but Rafi's firm grip steadied her. Their eyes locked.

No-one had ever said those words to her before. Well, no-one had ever said them in such a silky, caressing voice.

Returning his direct gaze, she asked, 'What is the matter with me, then?' She was no longer interested in what the village thought of her. All she wanted was to hear Rafi's opinion. Would he say those magic words again?

'Nothing. It is the first time a foreigner has found the coin, that's all.'

'People marry foreigners, don't they? You did.' In her relaxed mood, Emily felt no shyness about mentioning his wife.

'That was different. I brought Marie-Jeanne here on our marriage. Our women have an expression for outsiders who marry into Taghar. They say it is like sewing a new patch onto an old shirt.'

'That's not very complimentary.'

'On the contrary: it makes the shirt stronger.' Rafi gave his answer light-heartedly. It seemed the party had made him cheerful.

The rhythm of the drumming changed, and two young men bounded into the centre of the circle. Finding it impossible to mimic their energetic steps, Emily shook her head at Rafi in a gesture of surrender. He led her to a chair, but stood beside her, continuing the conversation. To be heard above the drumming, he turned toward her, and she looked up at him, her ears attuned to that caressing voice.

'If a young woman from Taghar finds the coin, her future is mapped out already. If she is betrothed, she will dance with her sweetheart at the wedding feast. But you, Emily, you are a foreigner: you are free as the birds in the air or the fish in the sea.' Rafi gave a mischievous grin. 'Sometimes change is not welcome. Freedom such as yours alarms our young men. They do not know what to make of you, so they prefer to make jokes.'

'Do I frighten you as well?' Caught up in the magic of the wedding, Emily dared to tease him.

Rafi gazed down at her. 'You have never frightened me, Emily. But I find you unpredictable.'

'I'm sorry. I get carried away sometimes.'

A rueful smile hovered on his lips. 'Don't be sorry. It makes life more interesting.'

Emily's heart turned over for the

second time that evening.

Someone began to sing. They both turned to look, and Emily joined in the applause when the song ended.

'What was the song about?'

There was an odd expression on Rafi's face. 'Why do you ask?'

'I don't know. It sounded mournful somehow. I thought a wedding song would be cheerful.'

'You are right. It is a sad song, a song of lost love. I shall tell Karim his singing touched your heart.'

'Tell me what it was about first.' Emily's curiosity was piqued. 'Why sing about lost love at a wedding?'

'Whether love is happy or unhappy, it is a form of madness — so our poets claim. The song tells of Majnun's undying love for Leila. Majnun lost his beloved, and spent his life wandering in exile.'

'That's sad rather than mad. He could have tried to find her again.'

That odd smile was there again. 'You mean *you* would have tried, my resourceful little Emily. I believe you would. But love is not practical and resourceful. Otherwise we would have no poems and no songs.'

'Songs aren't real. Life is real. Look at Asmaa and Mourad. They're real. And they are happy.' Emily indicated the bride and groom, sitting side by side on a raised sofa.

'They are married. Marriage is based on respect and the family.'

All afternoon, Emily had seen for herself the proud, fond smiles on the couple's faces. Whatever Rafi's views, Emily refused to believe that theirs was solely a marriage of convenience.

'Doesn't love have any place in marriage?'

'Of course. Marriage tames love. It is outside marriage that love is dangerous, Emily. That is what our poets teach us. Love drives a man to defy his parents. Love drives a man to fight his best friend. Love is ungovernable, and love must be tamed, before it drives a man crazy, like it did Majnun.'

Emily looked at him askance, almost

ready to believe him. The tambourines and drums, the dancing and the colourful robes of the guests, had all created a heady, magical atmosphere where anything was possible. Rafi and Samira would marry, bringing land and families together. But his heart might direct him elsewhere. To a wild, lawless land of dreams where love ruled and the customs of his culture held no sway.

Was there a place for her in his dreams? Her heart leaped at the thought.

An estate worker came up to lead her into the circle of dancers. The spell was broken.

Rafi did not dance with her again, although he led everyone else onto the floor, from the bride to the oldest grandmother.

Even so, his words echoed in Emily's ears all evening until she tumbled into her narrow bed, drunk on nothing stronger than happiness.

★   ★   ★

Sleep eluded Rafi. He recalled how enticing Emily had looked, her cheeks flushed from dancing, the blue of her eyes enhanced by her unusual pendant. He was pleased to have found a suitable gift to mark his appreciation of her. Much as he desired to watch over her, Emily was too obstinate, too self-reliant — in a word, too European. If she refused to discuss her problems with him, her misguided sense of independence might have driven her to refuse a more personal memento.

What kept him awake was not so much the image of Emily, but the flames of jealousy on seeing her dance with half the village. He had had to restrain himself from dragging her away into a corner. Jealousy was a disturbing, irrational emotion, which challenged his well-ordered life. He was long past the age when young men cracked jokes to conceal their anxiety at the changes sweeping Morocco. He was long past the age when lovesick lads consoled themselves by comparing their own setbacks with those of the legendary lover Majnun.

He was a man of standing. Old enough and wise enough to know his own mind. What he definitely did not want was his life turned upside down, however enticing Emily had looked with her red hair flying loose on the dance floor.

And if he did not want that, he had no business feeling possessive. Especially not towards a young woman who looked to him for protection. Rafi reviewed his conduct toward his young guest. Aware that one day Emily would return home, and marry someone of her own country, he had buried his attraction to her so deep he almost managed to forget it. Uppermost in his mind was the need to watch over her.

His feelings were not irrational, he concluded. He was protective, not possessive.

So why the searing jealousy?

7

Samira stayed on in Taghar after the wedding. A couple of days after Rafi left on a business trip, she entered in a swirl of floating draperies. 'Emily, darling, you will be so pleased. I have found you a job.'

Emily stared at her in amazement. 'I don't want another job.'

'Of course you do, darling. Nour here is far too old for a nursemaid, aren't you?'

'Emily teaches me English,' Nour retaliated.

'Yes, but we all know your father invented that job. He had to do something about Sofia's problem.' She turned to Emily. 'It will be perfect for you. My cousin has a friend whose husband works in Rabat, in the diplomatic service. They speak English and they entertain often. But she has two little children. They are

168

aged three and five, just the age to drive her crazy. So I tell her about you, and how there is no place for you here, and we decide that you can start with her next week. My driver will take you.'

Emily saw Nour staring at Samira open-mouthed. There would be no help there. Nour had been reared in the tradition of respecting her elders. However uninhibited her comments behind Samira's back, she was outwardly docile.

There was no way Emily was going to let Samira walk in and dictate her life. 'I will talk to Mr. Hassan. He is my employer.' She would tell Rafi she had no wish to leave.

'My cousin leaves the matter to me.' Samira pouted. 'Naturally he could not abandon you in Casablanca. But it needed a woman, such as myself, to find a suitable solution.'

Emily was torn between fury and despair. She thought of the complex webs of cousinship that underpinned Moroccan life. In Casablanca, Rafi had stepped in to act for Sofia Cherif. Now he had asked Samira to step in and act on his behalf.

'And, of course, if you are worried about the money, Elsa, you need not be. I am sure that my friend will pay you whatever is correct.'

Even the mention of money failed to rouse Emily from shock. Money was the reason she had come to Morocco. She worked out her finances every month, keeping a running total of the amount that went into the bank while the timeless days flew by in Taghar.

Lately, there had been another reason to keep an eye on her finances. As she closed her eyes at night, knowing that Rafi would weave in and out of her dreams, she also knew she could face him with her head held high. She was no longer an impoverished traveller shrugging off responsibility for the morrow. Instead, she had set a course that would steer her out of financial trouble.

She injected resolve into her voice. 'I will talk to Mr. Hassan first.'

'Darling, my cousin and I, we only

want what is best for you.' Samira's possessive words brought her down to earth.

Rafi would never belong to her. He belonged to Samira. He had given Samira permission to act for him.

Too agitated to go for her usual walk, she paced up and down her bedroom. At one stage, she pulled out her empty suitcase, before realizing it would take no more than a few minutes to pack her meagre belongings. The suitcase was a reminder of her former rootless life. The life she thought she had laid to rest here in Taghar, Taghar had given her a sense of belonging. *I'm staying*, she resolved, bruising her toes as she kicked the case back under the bed. It hit the wall with a thud.

But, no matter how she turned matters over in her mind, she could see no avenue of escape.

Rafi doesn't want me here. That hurt. Her fingers felt for the glass pendant around her neck, in the bitter knowledge that it was a gift of farewell, not friendship. Rafi would never simply dismiss her. That was not the Moroccan way. As a conscientious employer, he had asked his cousin to make alternative arrangements.

If Rafi did not want her, Emily knew she wanted another job here in magical Morocco. Yet the uncomplicated spirit of adventure that had carried her overseas had vanished. Rafi's company had changed her, to an extent that she would never have imagined possible. She had never before met anyone who lived his life according to a set of principles. However old-fashioned and rigid they appeared to her, they gave his family life a structure that had been lacking in hers.

There was so much at stake.

Hannah! She would ring Hannah. Hannah was a serene, rational person. She was someone people turned to in a crisis. Yes, Hannah would help.

Emily had switched her phone on before she realized what she was doing. *No network*, the screen informed her.

Her thoughts were in such turmoil she had forgotten about the lack of reception down in the bay.

How had Samira got in touch with her so-called friend? The thought stopped Emily dead. Had Samira left the village yesterday? Had her driver taken her up to the little town on the main road, or even into Agadir, somewhere where a mobile phone would work?

If she had not, then the sudden job offer was part of a carefully contrived plot. Emily seethed at the woman's duplicity. If Samira wanted to make a fool of her, she would have a fight on her hands.

Emily sprang up, determined to settle the matter in her own mind. The thought that Samira wished to be rid of her, as she would wish to be rid of any female under Rafi's roof, was one thing. The thought that there was deliberate malice behind her actions was another. The possibility that Rafi did want her, and had somehow revealed his true feelings to Samira, took Emily's breath away. She must find out the truth.

173

She needed to hear Rafi's version of events, longed to hear his voice. In a fever of impatience, she convinced the aunties to organize a shopping trip to the market town up on the main road. Finding a spot where her mobile phone worked, the news that Rafi was not in his hotel hit her like a slap in the face.

'Please tell him Emily Ryan needs to speak to him urgently,' she stammered, before clicking the phone off. Her thoughts ran in circles. Even if Rafi got the message, how could he contact her? Could he intervene in time? Did he want to intervene?

Why didn't he defend me?

★ ★ ★

No message came. Desolation trickled into her soul.

'I told you she is cow.' Nour's opinion was no help to Emily, who woke every morning dreading what the day would bring.

Her release was to walk on the beach,

pretending to look for pebbles. As she picked them up, the henna motifs on her hands mocked her. By the time the stain faded, Rafi and Taghar would be only a memory.

Everything in Emily rebelled at the thought. Chance had brought her here, and she did not want chance to sweep her away again. There was Rafi: Rafi who stalked her daydreams; Rafi, with those striking green eyes in his lean, dark face.

There was also Nour: Nour, who had lost her reserve and treated her as an ally since Samira's arrival. Rafi and Meriam saw Nour as a child still. *I'm the only one who knows about Nassim. If I leave now, I won't have a chance to tell Rafi — and he needs to know.* That secret weighed heavy on Emily's conscience, but the more time passed, the more difficult it was to tell him.

Beyond Rafi and Nour, something in Taghar itself had healed her. It had tamed the restlessness that once drove her onward. *What happened to my spirit of adventure?* She reviewed her travels across America. *Getting to know my dad's country*, she had called it. In reality, she had zigzagged across that vast land with no sense of purpose, to escape the disappointment of not finding her father. Sure, she had memories, but they were not the memories she had hoped to find in America.

Could I settle down here? Here, where nothing ever happens? In her heart, she knew the answer.

She was about to step over a log stranded by the previous tide, when she noticed scratches on it. Kneeling to rub away the sand, she deciphered the initials NA, followed by a date. Crude, uneven lettering, probably carved with a penknife, but not in Arabic script. She smiled, and imagined a child posting his message into the sea.

How far had it come? Emily frowned and tried to remember what countries lay south of Morocco. There was Mauritania, but that was also an Arab country. Further down the coast, her mental picture became hazy. Somewhere down there was Nigeria . . . but what about all the others in between? It was no good; geography had never been her strong point.

On impulse, Emily nudged the log back into the waves, hoping it would float all the way to America and delight some child there. It reminded her that the ocean linked Taghar to the world.

* * *

Aware that Samira's driver might turn up to collect her at any moment, Emily refused to give Samira the satisfaction of seeing her upset. Giving herself a manicure and wearing her best skirt became a form of armour, allowing her to be civil to the older woman when they met.

Other days, she lay awake at night. When sleep eluded her, she paced the room in the dark. *Why doesn't he get in touch?* she asked herself repeatedly, unwilling to face the fact that Rafi had left matters in Samira's hands.

Quite another event gave Emily her reprieve. Samira swept in a few days later, visibly miffed. 'It is so annoying. Darling Emily, you will be disappointed, I know.'

'Why? What's happened?'

'My cousin's friend's children have measles. It is the most inconvenient time they choose to be ill, those children.'

Emily gasped with relief. 'I can't go, then.'

'No. My cousin's friend is a devoted mother. She insists on looking after them herself.' Samira's nose wrinkled, expressing her opinion of devoted mothers. 'She says you will be more a nuisance than a help.' She shrugged her shoulders. 'We must think again what to do with you.'

She flounced into the kitchen to interfere in Meriam's arrangements for the day, while Emily fled to her room and allowed relief to overwhelm her. She would see Rafi again.

★ ★ ★

Rafi did not return, and Samira departed as suddenly as she had arrived, announcing that business called her to Agadir.

'What business?' Emily asked Nour.

'Import-export. Her husband was a rich man, but he had no sons to carry on the business. Papa says she has a man's brain.'

'I suppose that's a compliment in his eyes,' Emily observed tartly. Nour took no notice. She was following her own train of thought.

'She has gone to Agadir to chase my father. Why does someone old like her want to marry again?'

Emily was startled by her naivety.

'My mother was just eighteen when she married my father, and he was twenty. Perhaps I too shall marry when I am eighteen.' She directed a sly, self-satisfied smile at Emily, which alarmed her.

'You have to see Paris first, remember,' Emily urged. This was dangerous ground. She disliked Nassim, but supposed he was genuinely attracted to Nour. However, Emily was sure he had no thoughts of marriage yet.

The sly smile reappeared. 'I shall marry a rich man,' Nour declared. 'He will take me to Paris, and I will go to all the best shops. I will have nicer clothes than Samira.'

Emily breathed a sigh of relief. Her words had nothing to do with Nassim. It was a child's make-believe. She felt a rush of affection for Nour and her childish fantasies. She hoped Nassim would let her down gently.

'And I will never invite her to visit me, but I will invite you often,' Nour added.

'I'll hold you to that! Come on, let's go for a swim.'

★ ★ ★

The days slid by, and tranquillity washed over Emily again. The first almonds appeared, green shells hidden under green leaves. The olive trees came into flower.

The fresh, salty air and the smack of the surf lulled her during her long walks on the beach.

She was unprepared for Rafi's arrival. Somehow, in the peace that had descended upon her when Samira left, she had assumed that he would be as pleased to see her as she was to see him.

His first words shattered her illusions. 'What's this I hear, Emily? You want to leave us?'

'No!' The denial was torn from her.

'I thought I was doing you a favour. When Samira told me that she had found you a job with her friends, I said no, Emily belongs here. Emily stays in Taghar.'

Emily's heart somersaulted, leaving her breathless. Rafi had stepped in to save her. Measles had been a face-saving excuse for Samira. So why his change of mind?

'Samira made me see how unfair I was. In Rabat, you will have company. There will be other Europeans — other young people. All the things you told me you miss here.'

'I never said that!'

Rafi turned in the direction of his office as if reluctant to discuss the matter further. 'You forget your own words. You told me Taghar is too quiet for my daughter. That means it is too quiet for you as well.' His words were decisive, his face stern. 'Emily, I will not stand in your way. If you wish to go, go.' He shut himself in his office.

She retired to her bedroom, but left the door open a crack in case she heard Rafi come out again. She tried to read, but found it difficult. There was a constant procession of estate workers and visitors claiming Rafi's attention. She heard banter from the kitchen as the estate workers stopped to gossip on the way in, and Meriam's heavy tread as she took refreshments in for the more important guests. However hard she strained her ears, she could not distinguish the one voice she wanted to hear.

She was short-tempered with Nour when the girl knocked on her door. 'I've got a headache. Leave me alone.' Emily had no thought to spare for anything except the dreadful misunderstanding in Rafi's mind.

Nour looked as disconsolate as Emily felt when the two of them found themselves eating supper alone, and Emily wondered if Rafi had remembered to bring his daughter a token gift this time.

'Where is your father? I thought he came back today,' said Emily, feigning ignorance of his movements.

'He has gone to Abdullah's house, to talk about the orchards.' Attuned as she was to anything that concerned Rafi, Emily picked up on Nour's discontent. She hesitated, for unless she had just had an argument with her father, Nour never criticized him. Nor did her sulks last long.

Emily took the plunge. 'Your father seems preoccupied. Is everything all right? With the business, I mean,' she added, seeing Nour's look of surprise.

'I am a girl. Papa, he does not talk to me about such things.' Her face crumpled and she looked even more miserable than before.

Emily chose her next words carefully, striving to sound neutral. 'Is Samira coming back?' She dared not couple Samira's and Rafi's names directly in conversation. Like biting on an aching tooth, she felt an irresistible urge to speak of the two of them, to probe further, but she had no wish to betray herself.

Nour scowled. 'I hate her.' Her eyes brimmed with tears and Emily patted the girl's hand. She did so awkwardly, having no comfort to offer.

Nour sniffed, but seemed to recognize the proffered olive branch, for she fetched the backgammon board after the meal, and emptied her purse to give them each a little pile of brass coins. Instead of her usual enthusiasm, Nour played in silence, and Emily made no further effort to initiate conversation.

* * *

She woke early the next morning, determined to tackle Rafi. He had overruled Samira. He had told her so himself. But her moment of joy had been short-lived, destroyed by his apparent change of heart.

She found him drinking coffee in the courtyard. 'I need to talk to you.' The words burst out of her and Rafi looked surprised.

'Please.' He stood up and pulled a chair out for her. 'What is so urgent?'

He stood close, face quizzical, hands resting on the back of the chair that he held for her. Yet there was a chasm between them. Emily's throat was so constricted she could barely get her words out.

'I never said I wanted to leave. Please believe me. It's the truth.' She searched his face for a sign of reaction.

'Make up your mind.' Rafi looked none too pleased. 'Samira told me you needed a change of scene. She told me

I should not stand in your way.' He grimaced. 'I forgot you are not one of us. I forgot a young woman in your position has other expectations.'

Emily was not listening. The mention of Samira's name had angered her, but the only outlet for her anger was Rafi, who stood in front of her.

'I would appreciate it if you did not discuss my affairs with a third party. If you have anything to say about my future, please say it to me.'

'You forget that you are my responsibility. I discussed my responsibilities with a woman of the world, a woman who has my family's interests at heart. You can have no objection to that.'

'I can and I do!' Emily flung at him. 'I don't need her patronizing advice. And I don't need your advice either, Mr Hassan. I can run my own life, thank you.'

'You cannot run your own life in Rabat or Casablanca. You have no family and no protection.' He flung his hands up. 'If you want to leave, go back to England. To your own country.'

'I don't want to go back.' She heard petulance in her voice, just when she wanted to sound strong and positive. Dreaded tears stung her eyes.

'You prefer Morocco. Who would not? You should thank my cousin. She takes great trouble to organize another position for you. In Rabat. You will be in Morocco still, but in a lively atmosphere.'

'I don't need her interference.' *Thank her? I'd rather thank a rattlesnake.*

The silence between them lengthened. Emily looked at the floor, not wanting Rafi to read the yearning on her face.

'I will be sorry to see you go.' His voice sounded stiff and formal. 'But I will not stand in your way.'

His courtesy shut her out more effectively than his previous tetchiness. She squared her shoulders and looked him in the eye.

'I want to stay here.'

She swallowed her next words. She had almost said: 'With you.'

For a fleeting moment Rafi's face lit

up, and Emily's heart leaped. But his words were terse. 'You women! None of you know what you want.'

Her heart plummeted again, hearing him bracket her with women in general. 'It *is* what I want,' she assured him fervently. 'Samira misunderstood the situation.' Seeing Rafi perplexed and irritated, she sought to finish on a more positive note. 'Why should I want to leave when Nour and I get along so well together now?'

'That is true,' he conceded.

Worried that even now he did not understand, she spelled it out for him, emphasizing each word. 'I want to stay.'

Rafi flung his arms up. 'Stay, then, if that is your choice. I have work to do. I have no time to waste on arguing with women.' He stood up and prepared to leave. His apparent indifference sent a bolt of pain through her. He did not care one way or the other. Emily felt she had won a battle but lost the war.

8

Some days later, the household was thrown into disarray by an unexpected invitation from Samira.

'She invites me to stay in Agadir,' Nour announced. 'See!' She waved the letter at Emily.

'Oh! Are you going?'

Emily could see Nour was torn. The attractions of a stay in the city warred with her dislike of Samira.

'It would be correct to accept, I believe, since she has invited me.' Nour paused. 'But she is still cow. It will not make me like her.' She danced away to show the letter to Meriam.

What about me? What happens now? If Nour leaves, there's no reason for me to stay. It was another of Samira's attempts to get rid of her. How ironic that Samira could see into her heart whereas Rafi did not.

She escaped down to the beach, finding it difficult not to betray her distress. All she wanted was to stay here in Taghar with Rafi and Nour. What she had told Rafi was true. She felt protective affection for his daughter.

The pink feather dusters of the tamarisk shrubs shook in the wind as she walked through the village. On the beach, the salty wind whipped at her face and hair, and sent the waves crashing down on the sand in angry breakers that echoed her defiant mood.

All that girl thinks of is herself, Emily fumed. *It hasn't entered her head that I'll be out of a job this time next week.* That hurt. Nour obviously harboured no sisterly feelings for her. Did no-one care?

She walked on, heedless of the surges of foam that ran up the sand to ripple over her sandals. *I'll cope,* she told the waves. *I've always coped.* She shut away the knowledge that she coped because she had to. Because there had been no-one to look after her the way Rafi looked after Nour.

She knew this time she would leave part of herself in the place where she had allowed herself to dream of a future. In the place Rafi called home. The tide was right out, and she marched towards the headland, intending to visit the little cave one more time, seeking to imprint memories of Taghar on her brain. Careless of where she was putting her feet, she tripped and parted company with one of her sandals, annoyed when she picked it up to find the strap hanging loose.

That she would have to walk back in bare feet seemed the least of her troubles. She retraced her steps, her thoughts spinning in circles. By the time she reached the gate of the villa, pride had reasserted itself. *Let them dismiss me. I won't let Rafi see how much I care.*

She returned to find him entering into his daughter's plans. Nour chattered non-stop, planning shopping trips and parties.

'Papa, you must tell Samira to be

sure to invite my friend Leila. You know, my friend from school.'

'Of course. But no more running away to meet her! You do what Samira says. Understand?'

'Papa, I'm not a baby any longer. Listen, to show you how grown-up I am, I'll come and help you in the factory.'

'The factory will bore you, my chicken. You'll be too busy having fun.' He smiled lovingly at his daughter.

Emily fought back tears. Neither of them mentioned her. *Nour is a big kid. I can forgive her forgetting me because she's excited. But him!* So much for Rafi's claims that under his roof she was one of his family. She pushed her chair back and left the table abruptly.

Rafi caught up with her in the corridor and seized her arm.

'Now what has upset you, Emily?'

'Nothing.' She tried to turn away, but he drew her arm through his and led her outside.

'There is no pleasing you, is there?

You scolded me for keeping my daughter a little girl. You told me she needs to see more of the world. Now I give her the chance to do so, and you sit there with a furious face.'

'That's not true. I'm glad for Nour, really I am.' Her voice lacked conviction, even to her own ears.

He guided her to the bench under the tree and stood over her. His earring flashed as a shaft of sunlight pierced the leaves and Emily's world shrank to the patch of dappled shade they shared. 'I listened to you, Emily,' he said. 'I believed you. There was sense in what you said. Now I think that you are someone who will never be satisfied, however much other people do for you.'

There was enough truth in his words to wound her. Emily rose to leave, struggling to retain her self-control. 'I'm sorry you see things that way.' The strap of her sandal worked loose again, spoiling what she hoped was a dignified exit.

'Are you limping?' There was sudden concern in his voice.

'It's nothing,' she replied. Responding instinctively to the note of concern, she slipped out of the offending shoe and dangled it for his inspection. 'I tore the strap of my sandal on the beach. I tried to mend it, but it didn't hold.'

'Is that all? You picked the right moment. You can buy yourself a new pair in Agadir.'

She looked him in the eye, daring him to deny their callous indifference to her. 'But I'm not going to Agadir.'

Rafi looked baffled. 'Of course you go.'

The breath left her body. The shock of his words gave her hope, but still she dared not fully believe it. 'There was nothing in the letter about me.'

'I thought you knew our ways better than that. It goes without saying that my cousin has included you in her invitation. You stay one month, maybe two.'

★ ★ ★

Emily was surprised to see she was indeed expected and that a room had been made ready for her in Agadir. It was at the back of the house, but it was light and airy, with a balcony that overlooked a corner of the extensive gardens. It seemed that she was indeed one of the family, even for Samira who disliked her.

It took Emily only a few minutes to hang her clothes in the capacious wardrobe, then she opened the windows, kicked off her sandals and relaxed on the wide bed. Looking around the room, she could not help noticing the contrast between its opulent wall hangings and the simplicity of the rooms in Taghar. In Taghar, she had practical wooden shutters; here, gauzy curtains were looped back onto ornate brass hooks.

Emily even felt undaunted the next morning when Samira tossed a heavy gold bracelet onto the table and asked her to take it in for repair. 'I want to wear it tonight, darling. Make sure you tell them that.'

'Will they speak English?'

Samira pouted. 'I forget that you do not speak our language. How annoying! I will have to give you a note.'

Emily thrust the note and the bracelet deep into her bag, and headed for the jewellery section of the *souk*. There was a spring in her step when she got out of the taxi. *Let her treat me like an errand girl. See if I care. She can't stop me seeing Rafi.*

She handed over the bracelet and explored the *souk*, losing track of time. She lingered in front of a small rug whose geometric pattern in dark and light blues stood out against an earthy red background. The colours reminded her of Taghar, where purple creepers vied for attention with the vivid blue sky. Eventually, the merchant's invitation to take a closer look became too pressing and she made her way out, making sure that she still had the card with the jeweller's address. If she lost that, she would never find the narrow shopfront again.

Outside, a gentle breeze took the

edge off the sun. Relieved to have delivered the valuable bracelet safely, she decided to explore. Already missing the sound of the Atlantic breakers on Taghar beach, she headed toward the promenade, but on the way noticed an Internet café. She settled herself in front of a computer, ordered mint tea, and wrote Hannah a long email. It felt good to be in contact with her again; although, as she told Hannah, after the warmth of her welcome in Taghar, it felt strange to be an anonymous figure in the city, just another foreign tourist writing home.

★   ★   ★

That night, Samira hosted a reception to welcome them. Emily, accustomed now to the slow pace of life in Taghar, felt overwhelmed by the sheer number of guests, all of whom already knew each other. Having noticed that Nassim was not present, she felt free to slip away. Nour would come to no harm at her cousin's party.

She found a balcony where she could observe the guests in the garden below.

'You must be Miss Emily.' The voice beside her startled her. 'I was sent to look for you.' His voice sounded young, and in the light reflected from the lanterns below, his face looked open and pleasant. 'I am Mohammed Khabir, at your service.'

'Hello. Are you a cousin of the family?'

'No, I am a customs officer. I frequently meet Mr. Hassan when he exports to Belgium.'

Emily smiled. There was something almost military in his clipped speech, and she could well imagine him in uniform.

'I was sent to fetch you to supper. No-one knew where you were hiding.' His tone was cheerful and welcoming.

'I forgot the time. The city looks so busy, even at night.'

He leaned over the balcony beside her, and they watched the lights of a ship as it steamed out into the ocean and changed course. 'It is heading north, for Europe,' he said.

'How can you tell?'

'By its lights. Red for port, green for starboard. I thought the English were seafarers.'

'Not this one,' admitted Emily, and allowed him to take her downstairs.

Mohammed proved amusing company over supper, and she began to feel at ease in the crowded room. The contrast with sleepy Taghar was pleasant now that she felt part of the cosmopolitan gathering.

She caught a glimpse of her hostess holding court and realized that Samira was not someone who would easily abandon her urban comforts. *Will she want Rafi to live here? I don't see him agreeing to that.* Emily had come to realize how much Taghar meant to Rafi. His roots lay deep in its lemon orchards and olive groves. She buried the nagging thought that Rafi might enjoy dividing his time between Taghar and the city, just as she herself felt revived by the change of scene.

Mohammed introduced her to a young couple who spoke English, and Emily was in conversation with them when Rafi appeared at her shoulder. 'I've been hearing about the earthquake,' she told him. 'I didn't realize that's the reason why Agadir has so many new buildings.'

'If you want to see old buildings, you must visit Essaouira.'

'We could all go next week,' Mohammed suggested. 'It would be an honour to show you around.'

'Excellent idea,' approved Rafi, turning to leave the group. Emily was disappointed that he showed no interest in coming with them. Her pleasure in the evening dimmed, especially when she saw him talking animatedly in the group around Samira.

* * *

The excursion got off to a good start. Somehow, she had expected Essaouira to resemble the dusty little town up on the main road above Taghar. She was astonished to find it a fair-sized port, with stout medieval walls enclosing a labyrinth of narrow streets. Her companions explained it had once been a major trading post on the route between Africa and Europe. In its heyday, camel caravans laden with gold or ivory from Timbuktu plodded the thousand miles over treacherous scrub and desert to meet ships that anchored on the Moroccan coast.

Emily's spirit of adventure reasserted itself, along with the uncomplicated thirst for discovery that had taken her all across America. Travel had helped heal her wounded soul when she had failed to find her dad. Travel would help heal her heartbreak now. When Rafi married Samira, she would take another job. She could use her leisure time to explore places like Essaouira that were steeped in history.

She would forget the man who had wreaked such havoc in her heart, and take life in hand again. So she plied her new friends with questions, and was thrilled when they suggested she have a camel ride on the beach later. 'We'll take your photo,' they promised. The old Emily, the Emily who would try anything once, relished the challenge.

★ ★ ★

Rafi caught up with them on the ramparts. Emily was having her photo taken, leaning against one of the heavy cannons that once defended the city against marauding pirates.

'There you all are. I was looking for you by the harbour.' At the sound of his voice, a tingle ran down her spine. The meeting was no accident. He had sought them out deliberately. Had he looked for all of them? Or just for her?

Emily disciplined herself to remain still. The shutter clicked, and she was free to turn to Rafi with a smile of welcome. He smiled back, and pulled Emily and Mohammed toward him for a picture, his arms lying for a moment around both their shoulders. Emily felt that tingle again, before the photographers changed places, and Rafi posed with his arms around the others.

Emily could not follow the banter between them, but her new friends walked away with a cheery wave, leaving Rafi to guide her away from the ramparts, down a flight of stone steps and into a maze of streets.

'We'll meet them on the waterfront for lunch,' he promised her. 'Young Khabir wants to look around the harbour, and I told him that he could catch criminals more easily without you.'

'That's not why we came. He promised to show me the town.'

'He would rather keep his eyes open for suspicious boats than look at old stones.'

'He certainly seems keen on his job. He talks a lot about it.'

'He is dedicated. Our country needs more men like him.'

He pulled her to one side as a laden donkey trotted toward them. The animal was small, but in places its saddlebags almost touched the walls, and they flattened themselves in a doorway to allow it to pass. It was the second time that day that she had stood close to him, pressed against the heavy wooden door, shoulder to shoulder, so close that she felt the warmth of his body and detected a faint aroma of sweat mingled with cologne. She gulped.

'Don't be scared.' Rafi misunderstood her reaction. 'It won't hurt you.'

Emily concentrated on the donkey, wondering if its load was as heavy as it looked. A shaft of sunlight caught the woven ropes that secured an untidy sprawl of baskets. 'I've never been that near to a donkey,' she confessed once it had passed. 'I couldn't believe what dainty little feet it had.'

'You'll see plenty today,' Rafi promised. 'My wife and I used to come to Essaouira often. I will show you her favourite street.'

'Was she an artist?' she asked, when they arrived in a street filled with galleries and craft shops.

'Marie-Jeanne? No, she never painted, but she had a good eye for colour. She came from the north of France, and she complained that her homeland was nothing but shades of brown and green. She loved the colours of the south.'

'I know what she means,' Emily exclaimed. 'It's the light, and the contrast the light gives.' She pointed through an archway. 'Look at those blue shutters against the white walls and the purple flowers. They wouldn't look the same on a misty day.'

'Even women do not look right under a northern sky.' Rafi's rejoinder startled Emily, but he sounded pensive rather than flirtatious. 'I have often noticed the sun here is kinder to women's faces.'

He's thinking about his wife. I might as well not have spoken. Disappointment flooded her. Rafi was not even looking at her. He appeared to be admiring a display of carved face masks.

'What did your wife look like?' she asked. If he was in the mood to talk about her, Emily found that she wanted to glean as many details as she could.

'She was dark, with beautiful dark eyes,' Rafi said, again seeming to speak to himself. 'People took her for an Arab — until she spoke her mind.'

'What do you mean?'

'Do you think you are the first person to annoy me by preaching your sacrosanct Western values, Emily? My wife was young and idealistic. So was I. We argued many times.'

Emily was disconcerted. It had not occurred to her that Rafi's marriage might have had its strains.

'We married too young. I see that now.'

'What do you mean?' She had been intrigued when Nour told her about her parents marrying young, but had assumed it was a love match.

'Our families wanted us to wait. But we were greedy for everything life had to offer. Both of us. And with greed comes impatience.' He spoke softly, still looking at the masks in the window, as if his thoughts were back in the past.

So it was a love match. 'That's a normal part of being young,' she offered, in a conciliatory tone. 'How did you two meet?'

'Her father was seconded to our customs force for a year. He brought his family with him.'

Lucky woman. Not everyone finds their dream and seizes it.

Aloud, she said, 'You can't have disagreed all the time. Otherwise you'd never have got married.'

'European women are brought up to speak their minds. I was too young to make allowances for that.' A shadow flitted over his face before he continued, 'When I remarry, I will be more understanding.'

Emily's heart constricted. As they walked on, bleakness tinged the bright day, and she ceased to notice the carvings and paintings in the windows. But his next words surprised her.

'We both assumed we had right on our side.' Rafi turned to her, his face rueful. 'Let's say we both knew we were in the right, even when we were both in the wrong.'

Emily did not know what to say. True, he had described his wife as a *little bulldozer*, but she had imagined that to be a term of affection.

'Marie-Jeanne made many suggestions for the pottery. It took me a long time to admit she had a better eye than me. I should have known better, for it is women who use pottery in the home.'

Between the threat of Samira and memories of his dead wife, Emily felt more excluded from his thoughts than ever.

'It was one area where she could help me, but I was too proud to accept. My father delegated the running of the factory to me when we married, and I saw it as my responsibility.'

'Marriage is usually seen as a partnership,' Emily observed tartly. If Rafi was going to talk non-stop about other women, she could at least voice her opinion.

'You misunderstand. I wanted to succeed for her. To show her, as much as my father, that I was worthy of the task.'

Another donkey padded toward them, its handler oblivious to the artwork on display in the windows. They stepped back into a doorway, and Rafi looked down at her. 'A man must provide for his family, Emily, otherwise he is not a man.'

No wonder he and his wife had argued. He was intransigent. Despite her years of self-reliance, Emily was impressed. Rafi's attitude to his family was part and parcel of the way he shouldered all his responsibilities. She wondered if Samira knew how lucky she was.

Emily mollified her tone. 'That doesn't mean the man has to shoulder all the burdens on his own. Marriage is a partnership.' Although she could not imagine Samira taking an interest in anyone but herself.

'Yes, in our tradition the man provides and the woman runs the house. My mother kept house for my father all her life. But the world is not the same as it was in my father's day. When I remarry, if my wife wanted to run her own little business, I would allow her to do so.'

The remark flicked Emily on the raw. They deserved each other, she concluded: Rafi with his superior attitudes, and Samira with her scheming.

'She might leave you no choice.'

'What do you mean?'

'Suppose your wife told you about her plans and just went ahead with them? Would you stop her?' She finished on an emphatic note. 'Marriage should be about trust, on both sides.'

'I see that you have not lost your habit of laying down the law, Emily.'

'I wasn't talking about you.'

'I thought we were.'

'I meant marriage in general when I said that about trust.'

'I see. So you are an expert on marriage in general.'

'That's unfair!'

'Well, tell me what you expect from a husband in your marriage, Emily.'

His narrowed eyes threw her into disarray. She could hardly tell him that if he did not want her, she would never marry anyone.

'Love, of course,' she stammered. Unsettled by his direct gaze, she said the first thing that came into her head.

Rafi shook his head. 'We are talking about marriage, not fairytales. Love comes later.'

His comment made her defensive. Rafi had married for love, of that she was certain. *Why won't he admit it?* Emily nailed her colours to the mast. 'Other things are important too. Like trust and openness. But they are nothing without love.'

'I thought you sensible, Emily, but you are talking nonsense. You have not even mentioned the most important side of marriage. What about children?'

Children. The word pierced Emily to the quick. Whenever she thought of having her own children, it was something that hovered somewhere in a nebulous future. Of course, she wanted children. Once she met a reliable man — and reliable men were thin on the ground.

Now Rafi had mentioned children. A kaleidoscope shattered and reformed. The thought of bearing his child sent a shaft of pure joy through her. She stared, transfixed, at his serious face.

'That is why we say it is wiser to seek an alliance between suitable families.' His measured comment hit her like a bucket of cold water. Surely marriage should not be so clinical? Bewildered and alienated, she failed to take in his next, soft-spoken words: 'Of course, there are exceptions.'

'I don't see why people can't fall in love first. It happens all the time in Europe.'

'I am not talking about you Europeans. Here in Morocco, we say that people who marry must be comfortable with each other first. If a couple get along, love will follow, and children will follow.'

He slipped his arm through hers and patted her hand. 'One step at a time, Emily.' His eyes were soft. 'Good marriages are built that way. And so is change.'

They strolled down several more streets, arms linked like old friends, but

Emily did not feel like an old friend. He had matched his steps to hers, but she felt far from comfortable on his arm. He had no idea of the sweet torture his gesture inflicted on her.

Rafi spotted a painted fan in a window and purchased it. Remembering the beaded purses he had brought back from Casablanca, she felt half-glad and half-disappointed he did not suggest buying a second fan for her.

'Do you think Nour will like it?' Rafi asked her, as they left the walled city and started walking back toward the hotel where they were to meet the others.

'I'm sure she will.' Emily hesitated, unsure whether to say more. But he had given her an opening and if she was to speak, it was now or never. She plunged in. 'I tell you what she would like better. Start treating her like a grown-up. Talk to her about the business.'

Rafi dropped his loose hold on her arm and planted himself in front of her, his eyes startled. 'What do you mean?'

'She could help you.'

'How? She is only a child.'

'She is seventeen. And she will inherit the business one day. You said yourself that the world is changing. You should start giving her some responsibility.' Seeing his astonished face, Emily quoted his own words back to him. 'One step at a time.'

'What is this nonsense? Of course she will inherit the business. But by then she will have a husband to look after it. A woman cannot run it on her own.'

They had halted outside a perfume shop, and the owner, spotting potential customers, greeted them from the doorway.

An imp of mischief prompted Emily to add, 'You told me once that I should accept help when it was offered. So should you.'

'I do not need help,' Rafi barked. The rotund shopkeeper lost his smile of welcome and took a step back in alarm.

'No, but your daughter does. She needs you. I see her face when she wants to talk to you, and you pat her on the head and tell her that business is for men.'

Rafi glared down at her, his lips narrowed. 'Do you never tire of telling me what to do, Emily?' By now the shopkeeper had abandoned hope of a sale, and retreated to his counter.

Emily exhaled her frustration. If only he would listen! 'Your daughter needs you.'

'Everything I do is for her future.'

'And you're so busy working for her future that you're effectively ignoring her now.' She saw she had shocked him. 'It's nice of you to buy her little presents, but she would be happy if you took time to explain the business to her.'

'She is not old enough to understand. She has just left school.'

'All the more reason to get her involved. It will give her an interest.' *And if she meets a few more young men in the process, she will lose interest in Nassim.*

An idea occurred to her. 'Why don't you send her to take an accounting course? Give her proper training.'

'What!' Rafi was on the brink of eruption. Emily, eager to press her point, ignored the warning signs.

'Send her to college. Don't look at me like that. In America or England, millions of girls go to college. It helps them get a proper job afterwards.'

Her comment tipped Rafi over the edge. 'While I have breath in my body, I will provide for my family!' he thundered. Passers-by turned to look, but neither of them noticed.

'But when she marries, she and her husband will plan their future together.' Let this patriarchal relic see how he liked the idea of his daughter escaping his control.

Rafi waved her objection aside. 'That is years ahead.'

'You said yourself, the world has changed since your father's day. It will change again by the time Nour marries. Her husband might want her to help him.' She saw that her words had hit home. 'Nour herself might want the chance to do a proper job before she marries. Like her Auntie Samira,' Emily responded, pointedly.

'That is different. Samira inherited her husband's business interests.'

'And continues to manage them. Successfully, too, from what everyone says.'

Rafi frowned. 'True. But I am not sure I want my daughter to follow in Samira's footsteps.'

Emily swivelled round to face him. 'Why ever not?' Seeing his look of surprise, she attempted to minimize her startled exclamation. 'Samira is an independent, modern woman. Isn't that a good thing? For the future of the country, I mean.' She had no wish to criticize her hostess openly.

Rafi made a wry face. 'I find you charitable, Emily, to call her independent. Me, I would say troublesome.'

It was the last thing she expected to hear. As they emerged into an open square, Emily blinked, blinded by sudden, dazzling sunlight. Dazed too by Rafi's words. *I would call her troublesome. Had he really said that?*

'Come, this way.' Rafi touched her arm lightly to guide her into the shade provided by a line of palm trees. Even his touch failed to bring Emily out of her daze. He had called Samira *troublesome*.

The square was lined with shop fronts and cafés. Through a gap in the buildings, she glimpsed the masts of the boats in the harbour. Yet Emily felt as if they were alone on a desert island. Herself and Rafi, who was taking her into his confidence in this unexpected fashion.

'Don't look so shocked, Emily. You must remember that I have known my cousin all my life. Shall I tell you a secret?' He paused, looking at her quizzically. Then he appeared to make his mind up. 'I used to hide when she came to visit,' he confessed.

'Now, Emily, this is our secret.' He held a finger to his lips, but above it his eyes danced with laughter. 'I know well my cousin Samira. When we were little, she was bigger than me, and stronger, and — as you have seen — she is bossy.

She always wanted her own way. So I hid in the hen-house until she left.'

Emily giggled, relief flooding her. To cover her confusion, she even came to Samira's defence. 'The word you are looking for is *assertive*,' she informed him.

'*Imperious*, you mean.'

'That's not fair,' she protested. She sometimes forgot how good his English was. In this case, he had hit the nail on the head; but, having defended Samira, she was now trapped into defending her own position. 'It seems to me that circumstances have made her assertive. She had no choice but to step into her husband's shoes.'

Rafi almost snorted. 'After she nagged the poor man to death. A sharp tongue does no man any favours.'

Emily sustained her second shock of the afternoon, and could not resist probing further. They had turned into a side road, and were fast approaching the striped awnings of the waterfront cafes. Once they met up with the others, this privileged instant of communication would vanish. Rafi would withdraw behind his multiple masks again.

'Surely all couples have disagreements,' she ventured. 'It's part of life. Isn't it? You've just said you and your wife did not always agree.'

'Disagreement, yes, that is healthy. Nagging, no. When people disagree, it is a sign that the other person matters.' Rafi briskly disposed of her argument. 'In fact, Emily, most of the time I close my ears to what my dear cousin says. I have no wish to be nagged to death too.'

They reached the water's edge, and Emily felt grateful for the breeze that diluted the heat. Giddy from the day's revelations, she sank into a chair when they reached their meeting point and gulped down a glass of mineral water, answering her new friends questions mechanically. All her assumptions had been stood on their head.

9

Emily floated through the next days in a bubble of unalloyed happiness. Watching Rafi and Samira out of the corner of her eye, she now saw how Rafi parried his cousin's advances. Samira, however, was impervious to snubs.

'Rafi, you will talk to the gardener for me, will you not?' she asked one evening.

'What do I know of gardens?' he asked.

'My gardener is lazy. He always tells me that this plant will not grow here or that plant will not grow there, when I know — with my woman's intuition, I know — he is unwilling to carry more water. You, my cousin, you have many workers on your estate: you can deal with one obstinate old man for me.'

'My foreman will talk to your gardener when he makes his next trip to the city. They are of an age, and your servant will talk freely to him.'

He held up a hand as Samira protested. 'My foreman will report any problems to me,' he assured her. 'Then you may decide what to do.' With that, Samira had to be content, and Emily concealed her smiles.

Freed from the threat of Samira becoming mistress of Taghar, Emily even enjoyed running her errands, for they gave her time to explore the city.

'My new sunglasses have not yet come — and they were promised two weeks ago. Emily darling, take a note to the shop for me.' A typical day, a typical request. Yet Samira had an Arab disregard for haste, and no matter how long Emily took delivering a note, or taking a dress to be altered, she never complained. Nour spent long afternoons with her younger cousins and old school friends, leaving Emily free to stop off in the Internet café to catch up on what was happening in the world, and to email Hannah. Telling herself that Hannah would never meet Rafi, she found release in pouring out her feelings for him.

Internet access also allowed her to check her finances, and she was cheered by the reduced balance that showed on her credit cards. Little by little, financial independence encouraged independence of thought.

Part of her job was to escort Nour to and from her outings. To Emily's Western eyes, that constituted excessive protection. Yet whenever she collected her charge from the house of Rafi's sister-in-law Latifa, the easy welcome she was offered recalled Taghar. In sleepy, peaceful Taghar, tradition ruled. Tradition, so Rafi decreed, demanded that young women be chaperoned. She promised herself that one day she would ask Latifa her opinion of Rafi's over-protective attitude.

Another sign of independence was that she stopped worrying about her limited wardrobe. Samira entertained frequently. At first, Emily had been self-conscious about appearing in the same clothes again and again. Now, she felt no embarrassment as she smoothed down the party dress a local tailor had run up for her, even though all the guests would have seen it several times already. *So what*, she thought, snapping her fingers at her reflection. *I look like a local*. The reflection nodded approval. Emily dabbed perfume oil on her wrists, and skipped down to the party with a light heart. Rafi would be there. Rafi, who closed his ears to what his cousin said.

Mohammed Khabir offered to take her on a sightseeing tour of the *kasbah*, the ruined citadel high above the town. Emily saw no harm in the outing and accepted. She was surprised to find that they spent only a short time exploring the *kasbah*, but understood when he parked the car in a spot which gave a good view of the approaches to the port. Mohammed handed her a small pair of binoculars before taking a more powerful pair out of the car for himself.

'I know what you're doing,' she said, as they scanned the city below. 'You're using me to put people off the scent.'

'Please?' He turned a puzzled face to her.

'You're using me as a decoy.' What had Rafi said? She searched her memory. 'You brought me up here to keep a lookout. But if anyone sees us together, they'll think we're just a couple of tourists.'

'Of course,' Mohammed acknowledged. 'It is my job to keep watch. And to do my job in the company of a pretty girl is a bonus.' His cheerful smile robbed the words of any flirtatious intent.

Emily took no offence, and resolved to explore the ruins of the citadel by herself one day. She busied herself identifying the city's landmarks. The shadows were lengthening, taking the heat out of the sun, and she shook her sunhat off, allowing the breeze to ruffle her hair. 'Are you looking for anything special?'

Mohammed dropped his voice, even though there was no-one within earshot. 'We have received intelligence that diamonds are being smuggled through

Agadir. Blood diamonds! From countries to the south. Diamonds that could pay for roads and schools. Instead, they are stolen to pay for wars. And there are those in my country who would profit from such a vile trade.' Mohammed's face darkened, as if his own upright self were under attack, and he resumed his scrutiny of the sea lanes.

Emily shivered. When Rafi had joked about Mohammed's passion for his job, she had imagined people bringing back a few extra purchases from abroad, not serious crime. She returned to her own binoculars in a sombre mood.

★　★　★

Rafi whistled as he prepared for the evening. His decision was made. If Emily wanted love, he would offer her love. He said her name aloud, tasting it on his tongue. Even saying her name made him heady with excitement. He would sweep Emily into his arms and keep her there. There was only one honourable answer when a man was possessed, as Majnun was possessed by Leila. Tonight, he would speak to the bewitching young woman who had appeared without warning in his country to take over his life and his heart. That was only one answer to the desire that threatened his self-control. Tonight he would offer her a wedding ring.

Later, he sought her out and led her to a secluded seat in the garden. The chatter of guests on the terrace faded, and the heady fragrance of roses lay around them. Other people were strolling around the garden, but a soft pool of lamplight on the path cast long shadows and gave warning of their approach.

They chatted amicably. Rafi was in no hurry, waiting for a suitable opening to say his piece. Until Emily artlessly told him about her excursion to the *kasbah*. Jealousy rose in him.

'I ask you not to encourage young Khabir.'

'I don't!'

'He has taken you out a couple of

times, I have heard.' Her shocked look disconcerted him for a moment, and he continued stiffly, 'Such things are noticed.'

'Samira said nothing,' she snapped.

Rafi shook his head at her ignorance. Emily had lived here long enough to know what was acceptable and what was not. 'My cousin is a wealthy woman. Few people criticize the rich. It is different for someone like you.'

'Meaning?'

'You are young still. You must be prudent, or your reputation will suffer.' Even in the city, Rafi was aware of the damage that women's tongues could wreak. He did not want his Emily to be their target.

'I'll be the judge of that, thank you! Remember, I travelled all around America on my own.'

He sighed. The comment was typical of his fearless, foolhardy Emily. She would take on the world if she had to, but she had no idea what she was talking about. 'America is not Morocco.'

'Exactly. People have better things to

do with their time than indulge in mean-spirited gossip.'

So she did know what he meant. He followed up his advantage. 'Here, it matters what other people think. And reputation, once lost, is difficult to restore. I am advising you, as your friend, to be more careful.'

'I'm quite capable of looking after myself, thank you.'

There was a note of defiance in her voice which upset him. Under the brittle bravado, she must know she needed looking after. He could not tell her that, though. Not until he declared his intentions.

'In America I had to keep my eyes open. I am quite able to look after myself. In any situation.'

'It was not right for you to travel alone.' Here in Morocco, he could count on young Khabir to show respect. What guarantees did other countries offer?

'But I've seen women getting the bus alone here. You know, the bus that calls at Taghar on Thursdays.'

Rafi grew impatient. Somehow the conversation had drifted until it had nothing to do with what he wanted to say. 'That is different.' He dismissed her objection as an irrelevance. 'They go to the market with their neighbours. The bus driver knows who they are, the other passengers on the bus know who they are. There is never any trouble.' Seeking to close the subject, he added, 'I would permit you to travel alone on that bus, should you so wish.'

He saw the scowl before he heard the words. '*Permit! You?* Permit *me?*' To his surprise, her voice was shrill with outrage.

'Certainly.'

'If I chose to go, you have no right to stop me!'

'On the contrary, I have every right.' The time had come: he took her hand and clasped it between both of his. 'Emily, I beg you to listen. I have something important to say.'

'Another patriarchal sermon on my wayward behaviour, I guess.'

'Emily, hear me out.'

'I've listened to quite enough for one night.' She wrenched her hand free and stood up. 'I've been making my own decisions since I was twelve. I'm not going to stop now.' She had her back to the light, but he heard an angry sniff. 'And if that makes me unfit to remain in your employment, too bad.'

Rafi watched her go, cursing himself for scaring her away.

*　*　*

Samira announced her departure for Casablanca. 'I am so sorry to send you home tomorrow, darlings; it is inconvenient when we had a big party planned for next week, but what can I, a mere woman, do? It is out of my hands.'

Accustomed to Samira's whims, Emily thought nothing of the abrupt change of plan until Nour entered her room as she was packing. 'She chase my father. She want to trap him. If he marries her, I will wait for the day of the wedding, then run away to spoil it for them.'

Rafi's opinion of Samira had lulled Emily into a sense of security. Apprehension flooded her again, not helped by Nour's posturing. What if Rafi forgot the troublesome cousin of his youth and saw Samira for the attractive woman she had become?

Yet, as she reviewed the events of the past week, she understood. This was Rafi's doing, not Samira's. He had lured Samira to Casablanca. Rafi disapproved of her friendship with Mohammed Khabir and had hit upon this way of separating them. How dare he be suspicious of a blameless friendship? How dare he reorganize her life in line with his old-fashioned, traditionalist ideas? Emily fumed as she finished her packing.

★ ★ ★

Back in Taghar, the days were marked by discontent and irritation. Nour avoided her. Emily, wrestling with her own disappointment, left her in peace.

Nor did it help that Meriam remained

on watch. In Rafi's absence, Nour and Emily now took their meals with her at the kitchen table. Mealtimes should have been cosy, but Emily sensed a current of unease beneath the surface. Although Emily could pinpoint no cause, Nour was jumpy, and Meriam appeared distracted and vigilant. With Rafi gone, time dragged interminably. She could not help wondering how often he saw Samira. More importantly, were his ears still closed to her?

Even Taghar lost its charm. On the terraces, the stone-hard olive drupes fleshed out, their green skins tinged with violet. Emily bit into one, expecting to taste olive oil. She spat in disgust. It was unspeakably bitter, as if warning her not to judge by appearances.

The gulf between Rafi's world and hers had never seemed greater. He liked her, yes, but he made it clear he disapproved of her. Her prized independence had stranded her between two worlds, belonging now to neither.

I should leave.

A few days later, Emily heard a knock on her window in the evening, just before suppertime. She was shocked to see a bedraggled Nour outside. 'Help me in! Quick, Emily, before Meriam sees me.' Nour was already climbing like a cat, and Emily pulled her through the opening.

'What's the matter? What happened?'

'I fell on the beach.'

'Your skirt is wet. And torn. Let me call Meriam.'

'No. Meriam will make a fuss.' That was something Emily understood. 'Give me a clean skirt and tomorrow I wash this one.' She discarded the garment as she spoke, giving Emily another shock.

'Your leg's bleeding. Sit on the bed and I'll bathe it.' Emily emptied the jug into the basin as she spoke, and dipped her towel in the rose-scented water. 'Hold still, now.' But the graze was less serious than it appeared, and Nour was eager to escape.

Emily spread Nour's wet skirt on a

hanger. If she hung it at the window, it would be dry by morning. As she smoothed it down, a small packet fell out of the pocket. The plastic wrapper smelt of the sea, and seemed to contain something hard and knobbly.

She took it to Nour's room. 'What's this? Did you find it on the beach?'

Nour grabbed the packet out of her hands. 'Yes, on the beach. I think maybe it contain something interesting.'

'Let's have a look, then. I'll ask Meriam for a knife.'

'No! Always she fuss. I want her to leave me alone. I want you to leave me alone.' Nour stepped out of the dry skirt Emily had given her, flung it across the room, and opened the cupboard door to pull out another.

Emily caught the skirt, and retreated. Really, the girl acted like a spoiled three-year-old at times, even if Meriam *was* nosy. The best thing was to ignore her tantrum. Later, on the edge of sleep, she remembered the mysterious packet and wondered what it contained.

★ ★ ★

The next day, Nour was ill. *Skulking home after dark in wet clothes*, Emily diagnosed, but lacked the vocabulary to explain that to Meriam. By evening, her malaise had become a high fever. Nour seemed unaware of Emily and Meriam, who took it in turns to sponge her face and body with cool water. The hours passed, but her temperature remained high.

'Doctor?' she asked Meriam in the morning.

'*Oui, docteur,*' the woman reassured her, but he did not come until late afternoon. In the meantime, the plump aunties invaded the household and took on the task of sponging the invalid. With nothing to do, Emily panicked. Taghar was too isolated. The girl needed modern medicine, not cold water.

Pneumonia, the doctor diagnosed. He administered an antibiotic injection.

Rafi's absence seemed a betrayal. Where was he? Why had he not come in answer to Meriam's summons? He was the only one who could take decisions about his daughter's care. When she heard his car in the evening, she did not stop to think. She ran outside and flung herself into his arms.

His arms tightened around her in reassurance, and her worry evaporated. 'Thank God you've come.' All would be well now.

★ ★ ★

That night, Rafi sent an exhausted Meriam to bed. He and Emily shared the night vigil. They spoke little, but never relaxed their watch. The antibiotics began to take effect, but Nour remained restless. Uneasy sleep was punctuated by bouts of confused muttering. There was no sign that she recognized either of them.

Rafi's face was gaunt with worry. 'She's trying to say something. It sounds like *wait for me*. Can you understand it?'

Emily was sick with apprehension.

She shook her head at Rafi. 'It's a jumble to me.' She took Nour's hand and stroked it, bending her head so that Rafi could not see her face. The unintelligible mumbling would not stop. If Nour was calling for someone to wait, she knew who that someone was. *Don't say his name*, she prayed.

Hours passed before Nour's laboured breathing eased. Tension left Emily. She looked at Rafi. His eyes were on Nour, but his shoulders were less rigid, and his arms lay loose in his lap. When the first glimmer of dawn filtered through the shutters, Emily shifted in the hard chair, stretching her cramped limbs. The regular rise and fall of the bedclothes revealed deep, healing sleep.

Rafi laid an ear to Nour's chest, listened, and nodded. Relief showed in his eyes as he straightened up and looked at Emily. 'The danger is past.'

He let go of his daughter's hand and gripped Emily's, raising it to his lips. 'Thank you.'

A wave of faintness overwhelmed her.

Partly from the long vigil, partly from the gentle way his mouth grazed her skin. She staggered.

Rafi's grip tightened. His outstretched arm now held her upright.

'Emily! Forgive me. I did not realize.'

'It's nothing. I'm all right now.'

'It is not all right. Come.' Holding her hand, he steered her to the kitchen, pushed her unresisting form into a chair, and set a pan of water on the stove. 'You too must rest. Sit there while I rouse Meriam.'

He opened the kitchen door. The fresh air revived her, and lusty chirruping from the trees lifted her spirits. 'Please, no. Let Meriam sleep. All I need is coffee to wake me up again. I'll go back and sit with Nour.'

'That is my job. I will keep watch until she wakes.' He made coffee, quickly and efficiently, and pressed a cup into Emily's nerveless hands. 'Drink this and go to bed. You look exhausted.'

'What about you?' His peremptory tone did not deceive her. Rafi must be as fatigued as she was. He was calling on all his reserves of willpower.

Rafi swallowed his coffee in one gulp and put the cup back on the table. 'I will sleep later.' Steely determination overrode the weariness in his gaze. He laid a gentle hand on Emily's shoulder. 'I cannot thank you enough, Emily. From the bottom of my heart, I thank you. Not just for this night. Meriam also told me how much she relied on you.'

'I didn't do anything.'

'You were there. That is what counts.'

* * *

Nour was out of danger, but remained weak. The doctor called again to prescribe bed rest. Meriam guarded her fiercely, fobbing off well-wishers with mint tea in the courtyard and second-hand news of the invalid.

At first, Rafi spent long days working in the orchards, turning up late for meals with dusty boots, and eating in silence. His face was lined with fatigue, and

Emily longed to instil into him her own confidence in modern medicine. She sensed that until Nour was up and about again, hard physical labour was his way of keeping the demons of fear at bay.

Gradually, Nour recovered her strength, Rafi lost his harried air, and Emily looked forward to their shared evenings again.

'We cleared the last of the diseased trees today,' he remarked one night. They had packed the chessboard away, and Rafi lit his last cheroot. The fragrant smoke spiralled above them.

'How long will the new trees take to grow?'

'Lemons? Five years or so. Double that to get a full crop.'

'That long!'

'Don't sound so surprised. I plan for the next ten or twenty years. What I do now should have been done years ago, in my father's time.' His love of the land shone through his words. Rafi the businessman was hard-headed and efficient, but Rafi the farmer was driven by passion.

'Next spring, Emily, I will show you how we graft the new trees. It takes a sharp knife and a steady hand. Then you will see the grafts grow, year upon year.'

They were in that delicious bubble of privacy again, she and Rafi. She allowed Rafi to explain rootstock grafting to her, grateful to sit in the shadows and look her fill on his lean, animated features in the lamplight.

'What about the olive trees; are you going to replant any of those?'

'If you want your grandchildren to see them, yes.'

'What!'

'Olive trees live longer than people, Emily; much, much longer. Some of them live for several hundred years.'

Wonder dawned in her. *So that's why they develop those majestic, gnarled trunks.*

'It takes twenty years for an olive tree to bear a full crop. Even then, they make up their own minds.'

She exclaimed in disbelief. 'You're teasing me.'

'Not at all. No year is ever the same. Sometimes a tree is bountiful, and sometimes it decides to take a rest and surprise you with an even better crop the following year.'

'You talk as if they can think!'

'You should have heard my father! When a tree was not doing well, he would inspect it a few times, then talk loudly to the trees around it and tell them he might have to chop the lazy one down. He claimed it kept them on their toes.'

Emily giggled. 'Did that work?'

'Who knows?' Rafi spread his hands wide. 'Each tree is different. Trees have their own wisdom, Emily. We can all learn from them.'

I should have realized that he never jokes about the land, Emily thought, prepared now to accept anything Rafi said.

'So what do you say to keep them on their toes?'

'I never threaten. I cajole. I get good results that way.'

Emily wished she could change into a tree and have him cajole her.

Rafi interrupted her reverie. 'I will choose a sapling to plant next year, and call it Emily's tree. You will bring your grandchildren to pay their respects to it, and they in turn will bring their grandchildren to help harvest the olives. When you are walking with a stick, I will tell your grandchildren how you knelt to plant it as a young woman. They will not see you as I see you now.'

The caress in his voice took Emily's breath away. Did he mean what she thought he meant? Could it be possible?

Sturdy common sense came to the rescue. *He didn't say 'our grandchildren', he said 'your grandchildren'.* His words were no more than an expression of open-hearted Moroccan hospitality. If she ever paid a return visit to Taghar, then her children, even her grandchildren, would no doubt be considered honorary cousins.

'Once it starts growing, you'll forget which one it is.' She kept her tone light.

'I know all my trees.'

'How?'

Rafi explained, but Emily listened to his voice, not his words, allowing his soft murmur to spin a delicious cocoon of togetherness around them.

★   ★   ★

One evening, Rafi let slip a casual reference to inheriting some land in the next village, and Emily assumed he was talking about the land that would come to Nour on marriage. The thought jolted her out of her daydreams. She had felt totally at ease in his company over the past few days. Now she stared in disbelief. Facing her over the familiar backgammon board was a landowner willing to sell his beloved daughter for a few more acres.

Emily tasted the ashes of desolation. The man she thought she knew had vanished. In his place sat a stranger prepared to sacrifice his only child. *I believed what I wanted to believe.*

She had to force the words out. 'Do you mean the land Tariq will inherit?'

Rafi looked up in surprise. 'That old story. Who told you about that?'

'Nour did. She believes you want her to marry him.'

That betrayed no confidences, and perhaps even now she could persuade Rafi that the arrangement suggested by his father years ago was no more binding than his father's choices for the estate. *I owe Nour that.*

'Certainly not. It is one possibility, no more than that. Who has been putting silly ideas into her head?'

'Everyone but you, from what I hear.' Anger coursed through her, replacing desolation. How could he be so blind to his daughter's needs? 'If you ever took the trouble to talk to her properly, you would have found that out years ago.'

'She has only just come home. Why should I talk to her of marriage?'

'Other people do. Meriam for a start.'

Rafi snorted. 'Meriam knows nothing of the world beyond Taghar. It is time

Nour realized that. In a year or so, I will send her to Paris. Perhaps with you, perhaps with my sister-in-law. Once Nour sees something of the world, she will stop believing Meriam's fairytales.'

Part of Emily's brain registered what he had just said, but the other part was too furious to react. The man was blind, so blind.

'She will enjoy Paris. But what about afterwards? Do you mean her to marry this Tariq boy when she comes back? Because that's what she believes.'

Rafi considered. 'If they find each other pleasing, I would not say no. He comes from a good family. You met his mother in Agadir.'

That distracted Emily, for she remembered a pleasant, vivacious woman she had met a couple of times. Nour's possible future mother-in-law was no dragon.

'What if they don't please each other? What then?'

If Emily hoped to catch him off-guard, she failed. Rafi's answer was unruffled. 'There are others. There is no shortage of young men of good family.'

'Tell her that.'

'Why?'

'Because she thinks she is obliged to marry Tariq.'

'Surely not? I know my father filled her head with it when she was little, but we live in different times.'

'Yes, and you should give her some say in the matter,' Emily snapped.

Rafi shook his head in puzzlement. 'Of course. When the time comes, I will introduce her to several young men. She may choose whichever one she wants.'

'Is that how it works?' Emily faltered, realizing that she had taken Nour's dramatic tale about Tariq at face value.

'How else? Who knows my child better than I? Who has fed her, clothed her and cared for her? I have seen more of life than she has, and that makes me a better judge of people. I will make sure she meets suitable candidates for her hand.' He reflected. 'And should she hint that she wishes me to invite someone special, believe me, I will know him inside out before he comes through the door.'

Emily laughed nervously. 'I would be quaking in my shoes if I were a young man. You might frighten them all away.'

'So much the better. A man who is frightened of his father-in-law is not ready for marriage. When I meet the one who stands up to me, I will know that my daughter is in safe hands.'

There was an odd expression on his face as he looked at Emily. 'Love cannot be commanded. The more obstacles there are, the stronger it grows. Would you not say?'

'I thought you said love has no place in marriage.'

'On the contrary. Marriage offers space for love to grow.'

'But in Essaouira — ' She broke off, disconcerted. Her memories of that day were of bewilderment laced with delight. 'In Essaouira, I had the impression that you saw marriage as a contract between families.'

'Sometimes. In the beginning. But

life is long, Emily, and love is like a tree that grows strong in good soil. It takes shape over time.' His voice grew low and soft. 'What takes years in some cases takes months in others.'

'I see what you mean.' Although she was beginning to see, Emily felt she had to drop a hint that Nour might not fall in line so easily. 'Perhaps someone of Nour's age would be too impatient to think that way.'

Rafi waved her objection away. 'My job is to find my daughter a good husband, from a good family. To give her that good soil. Once she is married, it will be out of my hands.' His smile grew roguish, distracting Emily from her concerns. 'Couples grow strong in their own way.'

Emily refused to let that lingering, roguish smile sidetrack her. They were discussing Nour, not the way her heart lurched at the merest smile. When Rafi added after a moment, 'Taghar has shaped me, as England has shaped you,' she felt acutely uncomfortable. Taghar might have shaped him, but she should have known that Rafi would never refuse his daughter a choice. She regretted that she had left it too late to tell him the truth. It was too late to share her doubts about Nassim.

On the other hand, she did not believe Nour had deliberately exaggerated the situation with Tariq. The girl was too eager and trusting for that. Emily swallowed. She had been too ready to take Nour's side, without challenging her story. Paradoxically, her instant dislike of Nassim had prompted her to give him the benefit of the doubt. If only she had talked to Rafi earlier, the whole misunderstanding could have been sorted out weeks ago.

Now she must remedy the mess she had helped make.

'Explain that to her. She still believes you intend her to marry Tariq.' Inspiration came. 'Perhaps your sister-in-law told her that too.'

Rafi shook his head. 'Any foolish ideas have come from Meriam. You have seen for yourself, Latifa is a modern woman. She was a teacher before they married, and certainly she never believed my father's word was law.'

Remembering Rafi's outspoken sister-in-law, Emily had to agree it was unlikely she would promote early marriage for anyone. She was still trying to work out how to redress the situation and help Nour when Rafi changed tack.

'It seems that the men of my family have a talent for picking independent-minded women. It does not make for a quiet life.'

Looking at his smile, Emily's heart did a curious somersault. Whoever he was thinking of, she longed to be that person.

She endeavoured to keep her tone light and not betray her feelings. 'Perhaps you don't deserve a quiet life.'

To her surprise, Rafi's smile broadened. 'In that case, we have to accept our fate. Let us say, I must accept my fate.'

'I don't understand.'

'Do you not, Emily? You, who are your own person, generous and caring?

Someone who can hold her own in conversation. A woman a man is proud to know.' Rafi's eyes were soft as he looked at her.

'That's very complimentary.' Bewildered by the sudden turn in the conversation, Emily had no idea what he meant — save that this was no friendly verbal sparring.

'Actions speak louder than words. I judge you by what I see.' In the quiet room, Rafi's voice was low and curiously seductive.

Emily sensed he was in earnest and felt a vicious stab of guilt. If he knew the truth, he would not say that. She had let him down. She had let both him and Nour down by keeping Nour's secret. The one secret he had a right to know.

She made her tone aloof. 'Actions without conversation sounds very boring to me.'

It pained her to see his startled reaction, as it pained her to cut the thread of this conversation. If she could not have Rafi's love, she wanted his esteem. In any other context, she would have treasured the flattering words he had just spoken. Instead, she tasted ashes, trapped by her guilt.

A flash of irritation crossed Rafi's face. 'I thought we were *having* a conversation.'

'Rather a pointless one, if you ask me.' Her tone was brittle again. 'If your mind is so easily made up, I have nothing to add.' She managed a dignified exit before tears overwhelmed her.

★　★　★

A sleepless Rafi castigated himself. Another missed opportunity. At work, he was in charge. So why was it impossible to persuade one stubborn woman to sit and hear him out? Granted, the thrill of the chase was intoxicating, and Emily was a worthy prize. But if he did not declare himself soon, her foolish notions of independence might prompt her to leave.

The situation was not ideal. In Agadir, under Samira's roof, she would have space to consider his proposal. Here in Taghar, their close companionship clouded the issue. He would put no pressure on her. He wanted a woman who came to him of her own free will, not from any sense of obligation.

He must arrange for their return to Agadir.

★ ★ ★

A few days later, Nassim brought papers for Rafi to sign. He addressed outrageous compliments to Emily throughout the midday meal, with the occasional wink to Rafi.

Emily was livid. How dare he pretend to be interested in her to throw Nour's father off the scent? And would Rafi take his compliments seriously?

'What do you think, Emily? I value your opinion as a woman of the world.' Nassim's voice broke into her thoughts. His voice stressed the latter part of the sentence quite unnecessarily.

She glared at him. *If he could stroke*

my knee under the table, he would, she thought, pulling her chair back just in case.

'I'm not in a position to comment,' she began stiffly. 'I've only been in Morocco a few months.' Surely now Rafi would notice how unwelcome Nassim's comments were?

Rafi did rescue her. 'Emily keeps her own counsel on many subjects.' He turned the conversation to the coming harvest, and Emily was grateful.

After lunch, the men retreated to discuss business. Emily vented her bad temper by taking a vigorous walk right down to the beach. The exercise did nothing to improve her mood, for the afternoon sun was hot, and she had to rest in the shade before tackling the climb up again. She was surprised, and displeased, to be waylaid on her return.

'Emily. Over here, please.' Nassim lurked behind a tree, out of sight of anyone using the road. 'Please, you come.'

Reluctantly, Emily walked toward him, and he handed her a sealed letter.

His smile was unctuous. 'This is for Nour. You are our friend, Nour says.'

Not yours, creep. She hesitated. 'I'm not sure if I can do that.'

The smile was replaced by a scowl. With a visible effort, he pasted the smile on again. 'Emily, please. I know what you think. That I am bad influence. I swear to you, I am not.' He looked sideways at her, gauging her reaction. 'Nour is young. Perhaps she exaggerates in what she says to you. But I swear I do nothing to hurt her.'

Emily wanted rid of him. 'Give me the letter.' She held out her hand. 'I don't want her upset. I'll give it to her later.'

That evening, Rafi seemed abstracted. The atmosphere in the house had changed. Meriam stomped around like a bear with a sore head, and banged the coffee tray down on the table when she brought it. Rafi appeared not to notice. Emily sensed that he had withdrawn into one of his black moods. What had that reptile said to him?

'Did Nassim bring bad news?' she ventured.

'I have been here too long. I cannot be in two places at once,' was his terse reply.

'No-one can. I thought Nassim was running the factory while you were here.'

'I rely on him too much. He is willing, but he is far too young. There are matters that I alone must deal with.'

'Can I help?' she blurted out, surprised at her own temerity.

In the half shadows cast by the oil lamp, she sensed rather than saw him deliberating with himself. 'No, Emily, in this matter you cannot help me.' He busied himself lighting a cheroot, and Emily thought the matter closed. Then Rafi continued, 'Someone betrays me. Perhaps someone in my own family. And for us Arabs, betrayal is worse than murder.'

Emily was chilled. It was as if Rafi had murder in mind himself when he caught the person responsible.

'Who is it?'

'I do not know. I have examined the accounts, I have asked Nassim to examine the accounts, and between us we can see nothing wrong.'

'There you are, then: nothing *is* wrong.'

'Common sense is not always the answer, Emily. I know inside me that someone betrays me. Someone uses me. I do not know how and I do not know why. But I will find out.'

'You can't just say that. You need proof.'

'Do I demand proof when I see trees growing in the soil? I observe my trees, and I know within me which ones will bear a fine crop. And now, I observe my business, and I know within me that something is very wrong.'

'Go to the police. They have powers to investigate.' Emily's mind ran through conventional solutions.

'If there is trouble in my family, it is for me to remedy, not the police.' His manner was implacable, and she felt sorry for whichever cousin it was who was fiddling the books. At least she now knew what preyed on Rafi's mind; although, to her Western eyes, embezzlement seemed a greater crime than betrayal.

10

Emily woke with a start. She listened. Through the first chirrups of birdsong, she heard unfamiliar movement. Then stealthy footsteps passed her window. She pushed the shutter open quietly and peeked out. It was barely light, but she glimpsed a figure disappearing through the lemon grove.

A thief. I must wake Rafi. But how? She shrank from the thought of marching into his bedroom. But Nour could wake her father. Yes, Nour. Emily hurried down the corridor to her room, but found it empty, the bedcovers thrown back.

Sneaked out to meet Nassim, no doubt. *You are so lucky I didn't wake your dad,* Emily mentally addressed the empty bed, rehearsing the conversation she would have with her errant charge. She debated whether to go after her or leave well alone.

In the end, she had no choice. All those gossipy tea parties with the plump aunties had painted a picture of the censure meted out to any young woman who dared follow her own path. Nour was not Samira, a rich widow who flouted social convention with impunity. An arranged marriage, even one that gave Nour a certain freedom of choice, was still an arranged marriage, and family honour was involved.

I must go after her. I must bring her back before anyone wakes up. It was not a role she relished. Not for the first time, Emily regretted her rash promise to Nour. If only she had been clever enough to find a way of letting Rafi know, he would have taken his own steps to discourage Nassim.

Six months ago, when she was new to Morocco, she would have been amused at the idea of Nour outwitting an irate father. Now she understood the constraints imposed by centuries of tradition.

There was no time to dress properly.

She pulled a sweater over her pyjamas, thrust her feet into sandals, and climbed out through the window.

Instinctively, she headed uphill. Nassim would have come by car, possibly walking down the last stretch to the village. *Gotcha*, she thought, as she rounded a bend and spotted the car parked behind a tree. She retreated back around the bend and stood for a few minutes, catching her breath and rehearsing what to say. *Be diplomatic. Don't make her feel like a naughty child.*

Nour and Nassim stood on the other side of the car, arms entwined, heads together. Emily called to them when she was some way away.

Nour jumped. Nassim swore.

'Come back with me now,' Emily pleaded. 'Nobody will know about this, I promise. I'll speak to your father. I'll help you. Both of you,' she added. 'Come back now, please, before anyone finds out. Nobody knows I followed you.'

'How convenient,' said a voice behind her. Emily swung around and found herself facing another man, this one holding a gun. 'We don't want talk.'

Nour shrieked, and flung herself on Nassim's chest. Instead of reasoning with the man, he pinned her arms to her sides.

The man did not lower the gun. 'In the car! Both of you.'

Nassim manhandled Nour into the back seat, slapping her face when she protested. Eyes on the gun, Emily followed.

The drive to Agadir was a nightmare. Emily managed to get an arm around the sobbing Nour as the car took off at speed, throwing them against each other. Up on the main road, the driver stopped. There was no chance of escape. He handed the gun to Nassim, with terse instructions.

Twice, Nour attempted to speak to Nassim. Twice, the driver barked an order, and Nassim swore viciously at the girl. After that, she subsided against Emily, shivering with shock and fright.

Emily tried to control her own fear.

Bile rose in her mouth, making her retch. *I must be strong, for us both.* With daylight, the villages would come awake. The driver could not continue at this reckless speed. There would be donkeys, carts, and buses. A speeding car would be noticed. He must slow down, and she would have an opportunity to open the door and shout.

There was no chance. As the car slowed on the approach to the first village, the driver growled, 'Down. Both of you.' Nour obeyed. Emily hesitated, but obeyed as the muzzle of the gun nudged her arm. *I knew you were a lowlife when I first saw you. Why didn't I trust my instincts then?* As each village appeared, Nassim waved the gun and they ducked.

★　★　★

Emily recognized the factory when they stopped. Nassim held the door open with a mock bow as the driver herded them inside. Despair descended. It was

Friday, the Muslim day of prayer, and there was no-one at work. *Rafi will think we've gone for an early walk. It will be breakfast time before he misses us.*

Any search for them would be directed to the beach. How long would it be before he realized something was wrong? Too long, far too long.

Emily felt the gun in her back as she stumbled upstairs and into an office. Nassim propelled Nour into the room behind her. Their captor pulled the telephone cord out of the wall and threw the phone out of the window. The smash as it landed on the tarmac reverberated in the Friday stillness. Then silence reigned again. The man thrust the gun back into his belt, carelessly, showing them how completely they were in his power.

When he left, Nassim's demeanour changed. He rubbed Nour's hands to comfort her and, after a brief conversation, she turned to Emily. 'It is OK now. Nassim will help us. He only pretended to frighten us.'

He's lying! Don't listen! Emily wanted to scream, but swallowed hard. She needed Nour to be on her side.

'What happens now?' she asked Nassim.

'You stay here, but not for long. I come back to release you.' He left, locking the door behind him.

'He's lying,' Emily burst out as his footsteps receded. 'You mustn't believe him.'

'But you heard. He only pretended to be bad.' Nour's face was still blotched with tears, but her eyes were radiant with hope.

Any talk of Nassim's true motives would send her over the edge into hysterics. Emily steered her to a chair and put an arm around her. Swallowing her own fear, she spoke gently, as if to a very small child. 'Tell me everything.' If she knew what Nour had got herself into, she might be able to formulate a plan of escape.

'Nassim, he save money for us, for him and me. He do deal with my cousin in Antwerp.'

'What deal? Drugs? *Kif*?'

Nour smiled. '*Kif*, no. Nassim, he is much cleverer than that. He make the whole plan himself. Is diamonds. Diamonds fetch a good price in Antwerp.'

Emily collapsed into a chair herself, her legs shaking uncontrollably. Diamond traffickers were ruthless criminals who would show no mercy. *We're expendable.*

She had been blind and foolish. If only she had shared her concerns about Nassim with Rafi. The words had been on the tip of her tongue so many times, and she had kept silent. She had run her own life for so long that she had developed a false confidence in her ability to manage any situation. Fool! Nor had her impetuous action that morning helped. She had led them both into danger, when all she wanted was to protect Nour.

The evidence had been right in front of her eyes, and in her self-absorption she had ignored it. She remembered the oilskin-wrapped package that smelled of the sea. She forced herself upright, ignoring the knot of fear in her stomach. Again, she spoke gently. Now was not the time to infect Nour with her own panic.

'You collect them for him, don't you? You pick them up from that little cave on the headland.' That, not teenage moodiness, was the explanation for the girl's solitary walks. A flash of memory came to her. 'I saw a military-looking boat leaving the headland early one morning. Was that something to do with all this?'

'Yes.' Nour smiled with pride. 'I give to Nassim and he send them to Antwerp. When he has much money, we will go away together. To Paris.'

With her dreams of Paris, Nour was easy prey for heartless criminals. It was a waste of time to argue with her. What mattered was escape.

Emily moved to the window. The car was still there, two floors down. 'Keep watch, Nour,' she commanded. 'Tell me if you see them at the car. I'm going to try something.'

She knelt in front of the locked door

and breathed a sigh of relief. Their jailer was confident he had cowed them, for he had left the old-fashioned key in the lock. She slid a piece of paper under the door and prodded at the key with a pencil. It fell with a thump that echoed along the corridor.

Emily tensed, listening. No-one came.

Slowly, she drew the paper back under the door, dragging the key with it. Listening again, she turned the key in the lock and opened the door slightly.

'Is there anywhere in the building we can hide?' she whispered.

'But Nassim will come back. He promised.'

Emily seized both her hands. She had to communicate her own urgency to the bewildered girl. 'The other man won't let him. You saw what he was like. He's the boss. We'll hide and you can contact Nassim later.'

To her relief, Nour's face brightened and she nodded agreement. 'We can hide in my mother's room.'

Emily did not understand.

'Maman had a room here in the factory. When I was a little girl, I often came here with her. She chose it because you can see the sea from there. After she died, Papa kept her room to be private for him, but to me he show where he keeps the key.'

Hope surged in Emily. If there was somewhere they could lock themselves in, they could try to get a message to the outside world. They might find a telephone that worked.

'Did you ever tell Nassim about it? Think, Nour, think, it's really important.'

'No, I never speak of my mother to Nassim.' She choked on her tears. 'We talked about other things.'

I bet. The slimeball!

She hugged the girl and tried for a bracing tone. 'We have to move. Quick! Before the other man comes back.' She crossed to the window and threw it wide open. In the corridor, she paused just long enough to lock the door again and leave the key in place. 'They'll think we escaped out of the window. They'll think we were desperate enough to jump.'

Nour led the way through a fire door. To Emily's relief they took the stairs upwards, not downwards, and stopped in front of an ordinary-looking door. Nour ran her fingers along the top of the lintel to retrieve the key. Her hands shook, and Emily had to take the key from her and insert it into the lock. It turned easily, and Emily realized that Rafi must come here often.

There was no time to think of that.

She was surprised to find herself in a light and airy room. No wonder Nour's mother had chosen this for her sanctuary. Shelves of bright pottery lined one wall. A treadle sewing machine sat under the window, with a box of remnants still beside it. Nour collapsed into an armchair, buried her face in a swathe of fabric, and sobbed uncontrollably, as if she had just realized the truth of their situation.

Emily cradled her, shushing her like a

baby, knowing nothing could heal the humiliation of first love betrayed.

When the sobs subsided into heaving gulps she risked taking her arm away. They were safe for now, but for how long? They had escaped from one trap, only to fall into another.

★   ★   ★

Emily took stock of their surroundings. The room bore an indefinable air of regular use and she could not help wondering how often Rafi came to sit up here. He must have loved his Marie-Jeanne to preserve her workroom like this.

In turn, Marie-Jeanne had loved her Rafi, and her happiness left its imprint on the room. She must have enjoyed dressmaking, Emily decided, looking at the cheerful fabrics spilling out of the box. She sent up a fervent prayer that she could protect this woman's child.

She scanned the room again, seeking inspiration. Where was her mobile phone when she needed it? There was no point in scolding herself. The lack of reception in Taghar meant she had consigned it to a drawer in her room.

A phone. Any phone. She turned to Nour in sudden decision.

'Where's the nearest telephone?'

Nour clutched at Emily's hands. 'Stay, please.'

Gently, Emily settled her back in the chair. 'You're safe here. Tell me where to find a telephone. You can lock the door behind me.'

Emily repressed a shudder at the thought of the men finding her. She had watched the ships steam out of Agadir's port, out into the vast expanse of the Atlantic. What was there to stop the smugglers throwing a lifeless body into the sea?

She crept down the stairs again and began her stealthy search. Door after door revealed storerooms: some full, some empty. She pushed a fire door open, recoiling as the hinges creaked, and stood listening.

Somewhere, a door banged. Angry voices

sounded from below. Their absence had been discovered. She took a deep breath, willing herself not to panic. *Find a phone quick.* She removed her sandals, padding along the main corridor in bare feet. Every step took her further away from safety.

At last. An office, with a telephone and a computer. Only then did she realize that she had no idea how to contact the police. In the months of isolation down in Taghar, life in the slow lane had taken over, and mundane matters such as emergency telephone numbers had been far from her thoughts.

It would have to be Hannah. *Be there, please Hannah, please. Just be there*, she prayed. But Hannah's number rang unanswered. She rang her mother, dreading recriminations and explanations. They had not spoken for two months, and her mother would erupt with frustration and bitterness before she was willing to listen. No reply from Mum either.

She switched the computer on, rigid with fear now that rescue beckoned.

Again, she heard doors slam below. *If I don't think about them, they won't think about me*, she told herself, although she did not believe it.

The computer chugged slowly through its start-up routine. *Come on, come on.* What if it asked her for a password? But no, the screen flickered into life, and she blessed the casual Moroccan attitude to security.

It took an age to connect to the Internet. She heard an engine revving and the screech of tyres. Had both men gone? The click of the computer keys was loud in the empty room. She stopped, heard only silence, and started again. Her sessions in the Internet café had allowed her to master the French-style keyboard, and fear lent wings to her fingers as she emailed Hannah:

Inform police immediately. Held prisoner by Nassim Mansour in Hassan factory, Agadir. Not joke.

She pressed Send. Who else could she tell? Her mother never used a computer. Her travels meant she had lost touch with many old friends and her list of contacts was probably out of date. But that customs man had given her his email address. Something to do with coffee. *Think, Emily, think.* Cappuccino? That made no sense. Mocha, that was it, spelled MoKha. She sent him the same message.

She forced herself to tiptoe back to the attic, resisting the urge to run. Nour let her in and they huddled together for reassurance.

★ ★ ★

Time passed. A car screeched to a halt below. Footsteps pounded upstairs, echoing through the empty building. Emily pushed Nour behind her, seizing a chair to defend them.

But it was Rafi who burst into the room, bounding over the chair that fell from Emily's nerveless hands.

'Papa!' Nour shrieked, and threw herself at him.

'Rafi, be careful, they've got guns.'

His response was to clasp them both to him, hugging and kissing them equally.

'Rafi, there's two of them against one of you. They'll come back.' Fearful for his safety, Emily barely noticed that half his kisses were for her.

'They are fled.' He pulled Nour closer. 'My treasure, Nassim stole only money from me, but he was a worse thief when he stole your heart.'

'You knew?' Emily asked, her voice edged with incredulity.

'I was a fool,' he whispered, turning his face to hers and holding her as if he meant never to let her go. 'I could see you disliked him. I should have trusted your judgment.' The tension had gone from his face, but Emily detected weariness in his eyes. Her hand sought his and gripped it.

'Meriam could see Nassim was wicked.' He kissed Nour's hair. 'Meriam loves you, my treasure, and this morning when we found you gone, she told me her fears. I did not know where he had taken you, but I tried the factory first.'

Suddenly, Emily understood the reason for Meriam's prying, and understood why the housekeeper relaxed her guard when Rafi was present. All the time, it was Nour she watched, not Emily.

I must thank her. I got her so wrong.

It was not her only error of judgment. Her blunders had put them both in danger. But Meriam had spoken. Rafi had come. The danger was past.

As they made their way to the car park, Emily began to shiver with reaction. Rafi noticed, pulled off his shirt and put it around her. Emily clutched the coarse material with trembling hands and felt its warmth, warmth that had come from Rafi himself. *We're safe now!*

Rafi found a blanket and tucked Nour into the back of the car. Then he turned to Emily. 'We have much to talk about,' he whispered, 'But not here, not now.' Emily heard the vow in his words, and felt the pledge on his lips as they touched hers. Softly at first, then passionately as he sought her response. As if danger had opened the floodgates holding back his desire.

He released her, and Emily allowed her fingers to explore his face. Faint swirls of henna were still visible on her hands. Emily smiled to see them. It seemed Taghar had known what would happen before she did.

She traced her fingers down his hairline to touch his single gold earring. 'I dreamed of this the first day I saw you,' she whispered, standing on tiptoe to brush his lips with her own. 'I dreamed of this even before I knew you.'

His embrace tightened and she melted against him, hugging the warm skin of his back, locked safe in the circle of his arms. He whispered endearments into her hair, in words she did not understand, although their meaning was clear. 'I haven't even thanked you,' she murmured.

'No, I thank you,' Rafi said, his grip slackening as he transferred his hands to her shoulders. 'You are my brave little Emily. I chose well when I invited you to Taghar.'

Typical man, taking all the credit. It would be a lifetime's work to persuade him out of his time warp where women were concerned. Joy rose in her at the thought. *We have a lifetime. We have all the time in the world*. She knew him to be stubborn and proud, loyal and true. Rafi was magnificent — and he was hers.

He had come to their rescue, as her heart had known he would, erupting into their upstairs refuge like a force of nature. The same irresistible force that was bearing them back to Taghar.

She had arrived in Taghar as flotsam. Life had tossed her at random onto that particular beach. Now the tide of her impetuous life had turned. She would be carried back to Taghar on an intense wave of love and belonging. She could not fight her destiny. Nor did she wish to. Rafi had taken that decision out of her hands, now and forever.

Knowing that Nour needed his attention too, Emily embraced him one last time, a lingering kiss full of hope

and promise. Her voice rang with
confidence as she said the words he
needed to hear.

'Take us home.'